"So, you told the truth— your fiancé is not a lover."

Andreas smiled thinly. "Perhaps he and I have more in common than I realized. I had respect for you also— once."

"But not for long!" Olivia bit out the words angrily, the memory of Leandi in his arms still painful.

"No. As I remember, my respect for you lasted for the brief months of marriage, and then you reverted to childishness and ran. You fled without reason, without courage, without faith."

As she stood fuming, there was a wildness about Olivia, a noticeable sensual beauty that made her seem brilliantly alive. Only Andreas could do this to her. Only he could bring out the deepest emotions. "Go to hell!"

"Not without you," he said softly. His eyes swept over her possessively. "Wherever I go, we go together."

PATRICIA WILSON used to live in Yorkshire, England, but with her children all grown up, she decided to give up her teaching positon there and accompany her husband on an extended trip to Spain. Their travels are providing her with plenty of inspiration for her romance writing.

PATRICIA WILSON

WILSON

the final price

Harlequin Books

TORONTO • NEW YORK • LONDON
AMSTERDAM • PARIS • SYDNEY • HAMBURG
STOCKHOLM • ATHENS • TOKYO • MILAN

Harlequin Presents first edition November 1986
ISBN 0-373-10934-2

Original hardcover edition published in 1986
by Mills & Boon Limited

CHAPTER ONE

'YOU'RE not going, Olivia, because I won't allow it!' Peter Challoner's usually pleasant face was tight and angry. 'You realise the risk you're taking—going back to Greece? You seem to have gone out of your mind!'

He stared angrily at the slim, tawny-haired girl who faced him across the wide polished top of his desk and it was clear that he had no intention of relaxing the fixed determination that showed on his face.

Paler than usual, her green eyes worried and clouded, Olivia Page moved from the desk to stare out of the window at the green of King's Square, now dappled in the sunlight of the late spring afternoon. The reflection in the glass of the window did less than justice to the beauty of that unusual face, the widely spaced, dark-lashed eyes, the thick dark ring around the iris accentuating the clear green of their liquid depth.

Her mouth was perhaps a little too wide, but the perfection of her lips and the tilt at the corners showed a girl who had once laughed readily. The straight nose, inherited, she supposed, from her Greek mother, and the determined set of her chin, added a character to her features that took them out of the class of mere prettiness into an arresting beauty that caught the eye and turned the heads of everyone who saw her.

There was no laughter in her at the moment, though, there had been little laughter for a long time, and her smooth brow furrowed in anxiety as she contemplated the enormity of the action she was bound to take, for returning to Greece was a risk of such magnitude in her present circumstances that had there been an alternative she would never have given

5

a moment's thought. She would have taken the alternative whatever it had been.

'Grandfather needs me. He asked for me, and even if he hadn't, I would have to go now that I know.' She turned an appealing gaze on the angry face of the man who had never shown any anger towards her before. To upset Peter was the last thing she would have wanted, he represented all her future happiness, but duty was still strong within her, too strong to be ignored.

'I've no quarrel with Grandfather. He was never anything but kind to me. He made life happy and secure. For a while he was everything I had.'

Even as she said it, her mind rejected the words. Pictures of Andreas filled her head—his laughter, his unruly temper, his protection, these were the things her treacherous mind remembered, not the kindliness of her grandfather.

For a second she no longer saw the green of the square and the cool sunshine of an English springtime, she saw the island and the sparkling waters, the trim lines of the *Anatoli* as Andreas taught her to sail, his tall frame tanned and perfect, his dark eyes laughing into hers.

Anger blotted out the picture and she twisted her handkerchief around her tightly clasped fingers in a blind attempt to erase the sudden pain that, even now, could strike at her unexpectedly. There were other pictures of Andreas, and she would do well to remember them if she was once again to step into his domain. He was nothing to her now, she reminded herself, no more to her than she had ever been to him. He had chosen his path and she had cut him from her life.

'Anyway,' she forced a smile and turned again to look at Peter, 'if it's Andreas that you're worried about, there's no need. He's not a savage.'

The memories that had slid across her expressive face

had not been lost on the good-looking fair-headed man who watched her closely, and he came round the desk to stand beside her, trying hard to stifle his own anger and frustration.

'Look, Olivia, I haven't forgotten how you were when you joined the firm two years ago.' He had never met Andreas Skouradis, but he hated him with a depth of feeling that alarmed his orderly mind. He hated to think that Olivia had once belonged to the man, slept in his bed, thought of him often, for all he knew. 'If it wasn't a savage who did that to you, then I'd just hate to meet somebody you considered to be a savage!'

'Oh, Peter, when I came here I hadn't seen Andreas in over a year, you know that.' She moved forward to placate him—an argument with Peter was the last thing she wanted at this moment, there were already enough alarming thoughts in her head. 'I'd just had a bad time—it took a while to get over it—then there was Nicky.'

Her hand on his arm did nothing to restore his humour and she wondered just what else she could have expected. Of course he was upset that she was going, he had every right to be upset, and why, for heaven's sake, was she defending Andreas? It had all been his fault. He was the reason for her lack of interest in life, for her deep misery. She owed Peter more than she could ever repay. Peter had lifted her out of the near suicidal depression that she had felt after Nicky's birth, a depression that had lasted for months.

Memories clouded her face and a fleeting burst of jealousy changed the expression of the fair-haired man who watched her.

'Yes ... Nicky!' He knew he was speaking harshly, more loudly than he intended, but every time Olivia looked like that he couldn't help wondering if she still loved that Greek swine.

'Just what are you going to do about Nicky? You run

the risk of Skouradis finding out—I thought that was the last thing you wanted?'

There were angry splashes of colour on his cheekbones, a light in his eyes that frightened her, and she clutched his arm in panic. He had never looked like this before, and she saw for the first time the edge of a ruthlessness that had helped him climb so high, so quickly in his profession.

'You know it is!' Her green eyes were frantic. 'If Andreas even suspected that Nicky existed, he would track me down and take him! Peter, you wouldn't——'

As quickly as it had appeared, the anger died and he folded her into his arms, a look of quiet indulgence softening his rather boyish face.

'Oh, Olivia, would I ever do anything to hurt you? I know what Nicky means to you, darling, don't babble on at me as if I'm threatening you. I'm only pointing out that after three years away from him, you're running a great risk by going anywhere near Greece. Skouradis might get interested again, follow you back and find out about Nicky.'

He could see that that particular idea was a non-starter as her face tightened and she moved from the circle of his arms.

'Andreas and I are divorced, we've been divorced for two years. As to getting interested again, he never was, except on a purely temporary, sexual satisfaction basis.'

'Olivia!' His face flushed with embarrassment. Her often open way of speaking reminded him only too well of all the years she had spent in Greece—the Skouradis influence, he supposed. 'I wish you wouldn't speak like that. I don't like being reminded that you've been married before, especially considering the sort of life Skouradis leads.'

Olivia couldn't help the flare of irritation, but she quickly hid it. If only Peter were not such a stickler for propriety! Was everyone like that? Had Andreas spoiled her for anyone else? Not for the first time, she felt a swift stab of anxiety. Suppose when they were married she hated Peter's lovemaking? He was a wonderful companion, thoughtful and kind, amusing and reliable, everything she needed, but she had always resolutely pushed the more intimate aspects of their future marriage to the back of her mind. Maybe she would have expected little, but after Andreas . . .

'I'm sorry, Peter.' She was back to the window, looking out at the people hurrying past, each one intent on the small circle of their lives and she kept her face turned from him. 'The bitterness wells up sometimes. Mostly I don't give it a thought nowadays, but this business of Grandfather has brought it all to the surface again.'

Her grandfather's illness had forced out into the open things that had long been buried. It had been a long time since she had wept for Andreas, a long time since she had wakened from her dreams shaken and unhappy to find that she was not clasped in his arms. Nothing would make her live through that nightmare of a time again.

'Don't worry about Andreas.' She turned to Peter with a smile on her face, holding it there by sheer willpower. 'The marriage was all arranged by Grandfather. I think that Andreas could never have been really interested, except that deep down he wanted what Grandfather wanted, all ends neatly tied up. Andreas is not really a Skouradis, except by adoption. I'm the only Skouradis because of my mother. A male heir was needed.' Her curious green eyes turned on him, a blaze of green fire flashing unexpectedly from their liquid depths.

'Neither of them knows or will ever know that the necessary heir exists. Nicky is mine! Nothing can take him from me!'

Peter watched her with a twinge of anxiety of his

own. She rarely showed anything but submission and gentle calm. Even the mention of Skouradis had been enough to put this fire into her, and he wondered uneasily if he really knew her. If he understood her depth of hatred for the powerful man in Greece who had ruined her life. He already knew the, to him, unreasonable devotion she had to the child, and his mind eased a little when he considered what a return to Skouradis would mean to Olivia. No, she was safe, she would not be likely to fall into the same trap again, not when she had Nicky to protect.

He caught her to him again, kissing her gently. She was stiff and cold, a hardness in her that was totally at variance with her usual nature, but his stroking hands relaxed her, breaking through the barrier that had grown between them, a barrier that had made him feel somehow inadequate in the face of the heated emotions that words and memories had aroused.

'Look, it's time I had a break. Would you like me to come out there and join you? You'll have to leave without me, but I could get there when the Markington case is off my back, say three or four days after you go?'

'Oh, would you, Peter?' She felt hope rise in her for the first time since she had entered the office, a renewed burst of confidence in her ability to face the inevitable meeting with Andreas. 'I'd be so grateful. It would make all the difference in the world if you were there.'

He threw his head back, laughing in that open boyish way that she found so attractive, generous and easygoing again.

'Darling girl! I don't need gratitude. We'll be married in July, it's only three months away. My place is beside you, of course I'll come.' He was happier now. Maybe it was a good thing, a chance for her to see once and for all the contrast between the stability he could give her and the turmoil that was all she would ever get from that hard-bitten Greek.

'Now off you go, darling. I'll be glad when we're married and you're not in the office any more. It's hard enough to work at the best of times, knowing that you're only a couple of doors away.' He gave her a hug as she went, and her mind was easier than it had been since she had received the cable from Greece.

Olivia's state of mind, however, was considerably altered when she came out into the arrival lounge at Athens airport the next day. She had already battled with herself, fighting down the memories of the last time she had been here, the time when she had been leaving Greece permanently because of Andreas.

She tried to stifle the anger and bitterness that threatened to surface again, but it was too close now, much too close. Her own unhappy parting from Nicky that morning and the little ache that still tugged at her when she thought of those dark, tear-filled eyes, only added to her resentment and anger.

For a brief moment she had the urge to turn round and go back immediately, ignoring the call from her grandfather that had pulled her here.

Everything she had loved had once been here in this warm, sunny land. All her dreams and hopes had been wrapped up in Andreas, but he had torn them from her, turning her into an exile, forcing her to flee from everything she had once held so dear.

Marriage to Andreas had been a dream that turned into a nightmare. There had always been a quality of unreality about it, always a suspicion at the back of her mind that she would wake up and find that it was all untrue, that someone like Andreas would never have thought of marrying an unsophisticated girl of eighteen. A girl he had called cousin for so many years.

She realised now that she had always been wary, anxiously watching for any change in Andreas, nervous when he was out of her sight. How right her instincts had been!

She struggled with her feelings, resentment mixed with pain, and the frightening little burst of excitement that came every time he realised that soon she would see him. The cable had said that Andreas would meet her flight in Athens and, therefore, he would be there, on time. He left nothing to chance.

Olivia saw him before he saw her, recognising him so quickly because he had not changed at all. He looked perhaps a little harsher, leaner, but apart from that he was still the same.

She realised with a swift stab of annoyance that he would be looking for the Olivia he remembered, tawny hair streaked with gold from the sun, hanging down her back in a silken cape, long legs slim and brown beneath short dresses, her eyes laughing and happy. What would he make of her now? she thought grimly.

He stood just inside the main entrance, leaving no chance that he would miss her, and she was thankful that he had, as yet, not turned his head in her direction. To think of him was one thing, to actually see him was altogether different.

The thick black hair, beautifully cut, brushed smoothly to his head, still just touched his white collar at the back. His superbly tailored grey suit showed the wide shoulders, the strong length of his legs, his slim hips as he stood, hands in pockets, his jacket pushed back, his head tilted with the same old arrogance as his dark eyes scanned the crowd.

Even among the good-looking men who either waited for relatives or moved briskly through the crowds towards the heavy glass doors, he was instantly noticeable. There was a hard masculine beauty about the stern golden-tanned face, the sheer physical perfection of a Greek statue about his six-feet-two athletic build.

Olivia could tell, as she saw the cool, firm mouth turned slightly down, the thick black brows drawn together in a frown, that he was no more looking forward to this meeting than she was herself.

Tomas was with him too. Another noticeable man. Not because of his masculine perfection, but because of the air of danger about him. He wore his power like armour, his eyes watchful and intelligent. Tomas had seen her already, recognised her and kept silent, only the quick lift of the corners of his mouth telling her that she was noticed and welcome.

He was big, in capital letters, not with the height and superb build of Andreas, but with a bulk that was entirely muscle and bone, not a spare ounce of fat on him. Ugly and dangerous—but not as dangerous as his employer. He was, as he had told Olivia often in her childhood, definitely no oil painting, but she had a soft spot for him that even now threatened to take the cool mask she made of her face by surprise.

Of course, Andreas never stirred without his chauffeur and bodyguard. She should have expected to see him one step behind Andreas. It was only on the island that he was free to move about without Tomas. Enormous wealth brought enormous danger and in every photograph she had even seen of Andreas in the press, somewhere in the picture, alert and watchful, had been the threatening presence of Tomas Polludrios.

Andreas saw her then, but any shock he felt at the sight of the cool sophisticated woman who walked towards him was kept well hidden behind cold, dark eyes. Her long hair swept from her face and coiled neatly behind her head, her slender figure beautiful in a cream suit and dark green blouse, she was as different from the warm excitable girl he remembered as to be another person. Three years had changed her completely, and the knowledge of this gave her confidence, allowed her to walk straight towards him, her head high.

He watched her, his cold eyes calculating her appearance. She was taller than the woman he knew, more slender. The eyes were still the same, still astonishingly green, tilted and dark-lashed with the strange luminosity of the sea, but her expression was hard, her hatred a visible force.

He gave her no smile of greeting, did not relinquish his position by the door, but the dark eyes pinned her with an intensity that made her controlled footsteps falter for one brief moment until she forced her mind to control her body. For one alarming second, she had been eighteen again, bewitched by those eyes, drowning in their depths, but her face remained impassive and the only smile she had was for Tomas.

'*Kalimera*, Olivia. I welcome my wife back to her own country.' Andreas greeted her in English, his deep voice sending an unwelcome shiver down her spine, again that odd mixture of annoyance and excitement, of pain and panic. His choice of greeting was a deliberate act of antagonism and she rounded on him instantly.

'I still speak Greek, Andreas,' she answered in his own language, 'and I am not your wife.'

She handed her luggage ticket to him in an act of superiority that was totally lost on him. He didn't expect a woman to do anything in any way businesslike. To shock him she would have had to wade in among the luggage and collect her own. That would really have angered him, and Olivia gave herself a mental shake as she remembered. Not that she wished to anger him, she wanted to see as little of him as she could.

Her only concern was to see her grandfather and get back to England as quickly as possible to her son—a perfect miniature image of his father. She stared at Andreas for a second as the uncanny likeness left her suddenly weak and bewildered, and also for a second, he stared back, his beautiful dark eyes narrowed

beneath the thick curling lashes, his straight dark brows
raised.

'You seem surprised, Olivia. What, I wonder, did you
expect?'

'From you? Nothing!' The words were bitten out with
more than usual tartness. She would have to learn to
look at him without thinking of Nicky, without
thinking of Andreas as he too had been when he had
laughed and wound his arm around her neck.

'Then you will not be disappointed, my wife.'

'I am not your wife!'

His tight lips relaxed into a smile. 'Constant
repetition does not alter a fact, Olivia.'

'I could well say the same to you!'

He faced the angry flash of her eyes with ill-concealed
contempt, his tight-lipped smile still in place.

'Possibly, but as right is on my side, I should ignore
you. Come along.'

He snapped his fingers, holding the luggage ticket out
over his shoulder to Tomas, before taking her arm and
leading her outside, his attitude remote and aloof as if
she were a recalcitrant child who had been caught
trying to smuggle herself aboard an aircraft.

The heat was a blessing after the cool spring air of
London and for a second, Olivia turned her face up to
the sun, her blood stirring at once at the sights and
sounds of everything she had once held so dear and
taken so much for granted. Her mouth relaxed into a
smile even without her knowing it, as she drank in the
warmth, the scents, the heartbeat of Greece.

This was her mother's country, her own land, where
she had been happy beyond her wildest dreams, where
life had been one long day after another of warmth and
pleasure, where she had learned how to live, how to
love . . .

'Like a kitten greeting the sun. I almost expect to
hear you purr, Olivia.'

He was watching her, a half smile on his face, his eyes knowing, aware of her sensual reaction to the ambience of the place, aware too of the memories that flooded her mind, threatened to engulf her.

She wrenched her arm from his grip, ignoring the swift anger that crossed his face and stepped to the black Mercedes that was parked at the kerb. She didn't need to be told that this was his car, the fact that it was parked in a clearly marked no parking area was enough to proclaim it as Skouradis property. He behaved like a king and everyone accepted it—expected it.

She slid in without his help and settled herself comfortably, annoyed that he had seen her moment of weakness, angry with herself at her reaction to familiar things.

'How is my grandfather?' She spoke without looking at Andreas as he slid smoothly in beside her, stretching his long legs out and resting his head against the upholstery of the seat.

'Still unable to move very freely, but much better,' he answered with the same remote, unfeeling inflection that he had adopted on her arrival. 'There was no need whatever for you to come.'

'Then why was I sent for?' She stared at him in real astonishment. 'Why did you send the cable?'

'I did not send anything, Olivia. The whole arrangement has been dealt with by your grandfather in my absence. Alex still possesses that certain amount of low cunning that you undoubtedly remember yourself. Putting my name to the cable was his idea of impressing upon you the seriousness of his condition. He has been very ill, a stroke is not to be written off easily, but he has recovered to a great extent. There is no danger now. The cable was an effort to pull at your heartstrings, and clearly it succeeded.'

'You've seen what he put?'

'Oh, yes,' he smiled briefly, his quick sardonic glance

flickering over her and then away again. 'From time to time he feels the need to confess his sins. He showed me what he had written.'

'I suppose you were no more pleased, then, than I am now?'

'Pleased?' Andreas shrugged elegantly. 'It is of no importance. Alex wanted to see you, which is a natural thing after three years, don't you think? That he had to resort to subterfuge is not, I believe, entirely his fault.'

Olivia bit her lip and remained silent. The subtle rebuke, the quiet reminder that when she had fled from Greece she had also fled from an old man who loved her, had been meant to sting, and it did. She might have known that Alex Skouradis would come up with some plan to get her back. When he wanted something, he got it, even when Andreas objected.

She had good reason too to remember her grandfather's cunning. After all, wasn't that the reason for her marriage in the first place? Her grandfather had a stubborn determination to get his own way and a very tricky method of going about it when necessary.

'You could have sent another cable and told me not to come.'

'And been at the receiving end of your suspicious little mind yet again? I think not, Olivia.' He did not even bother to look at her. 'You are here, and you will see Alex tomorrow.'

'Tomorrow?' She turned resentful eyes on him. 'What's wrong with today? It's still early. What's to prevent me from going out to the island today?'

'I am preventing you, Olivia!' He turned, and under the punishing stare of the night-black eyes she fell silent. 'I shall be escorting you to Illyaros myself, but my business in Athens is not yet completed. Therefore you will see your grandfather tomorrow.'

'I see.' Olivia turned away, fuming with frustration, unable to meet those eyes any longer. 'For one moment

I forgot that I was back in Greece and therefore suddenly incapable of managing my own affairs. I do apologise, Andreas.'

She looked out of the window to catch her first glimpse of the city in three years, forcing her mind to ignore him, to forget the vibrant aggressive figure who leaned with deceptive ease beside her. She knew him well, he could turn from languid contemplation of the city, to violent anger in seconds.

There was an electric current of hatred passing between them though they faced in opposite directions, and Tomas, easing himself into the driving seat, slid the heavy glass partition closed, thus shutting them into the angry silence at the back of the car. Tomas' dark eyes caught Olivia's gaze. She knew what he was thinking. This was what he had expected, but not what he had hoped for.

She saw him grimace to himself as he brought the purring motor to life. The days would be black again, he thought, as black as they had been before. It would have been better for things to stay as they were.

'Where are we staying?' Olivia's tight question came after a long silence. The strained atmosphere seemed to have no effect upon Andreas, but Olivia found it suddenly unbearable.

'I am staying at the apartment, naturally.' He did not look round. 'Equally naturally, I imagined that you would not wish to stay there. I've booked you a suite at the Meridien.'

Olivia clenched her gloved hands together. No, she did not wish to stay at the apartment. Even the mention of it brought pain to the pit of her stomach. The last time she had been there she had been packing, throwing the few clothes she had brought with her into a suitcase, Andreas pleading with her and finally storming out of the door. She had never gone back to Illyaros, she had been in England by nightfall, racing to the comfort and sympathy of her Aunt Beth, her father's only sister.

No, she certainly did not want to stay at the apartment, she never wanted to see it again.

Anger tore through her like a fire. All this meant nothing to him, and the feeling of regret that she had suffered when she had seen him, when she had stopped, stricken and bewildered at the likeness between Nicky and his arrogant father, was drowned in bitterness. She knew who would stay at the apartment now.

'Do you think it will suit you, Olivia?' His voice was stony. 'It is a very luxurious hotel. There's a pool where you can swim this afternoon. I shall be busy,' he added unnecessarily.

'It will suit me very well, Andreas.' She turned a cool look on him and found his eyes on her broodingly. 'However, I shall shop this afternoon.'

'You will not!' His hand shot out and grasped her wrist, her quiet sentence bringing him to aggressive action immediately. 'You will stay safely in the hotel until I collect you for dinner. I have many enemies and no doubt your arrival has been noted by them all.'

'Why should they bother with me?' She tried vainly to remove her wrist from the steel clamp of his fingers.

'Don't be stupid, Olivia!' he bit out harshly. 'You are my wife. What other reason would they need?'

'I'm not your wife!' She was shouting now, uncaring as to whether Tomas heard or not. 'Let me remind you for the last time that we're divorced! All the papers were served on you and you received notification when the divorce became final.'

'Yes. A long envelope and a cold legal document in quaint English. In it, I remember, you were called "the aforementioned". I received it, Olivia, and consigned it immediately to the fire. Call yourself whatever you wish in England. Here you are my wife!' His eyes slid over her in sardonic appraisal. 'If I so wished, I could claim the rights that have been denied me for so long.'

Olivia stared at him in shocked silence, totally at a

loss for words, but he released her hand with an angry shrug and turned away from the increased pallor of her face.

'Don't alarm yourself. I'm no longer interested.' He shot her a threatening look from under lowered dark brows. 'I told you that a suite has been reserved for you at the Meridien. Stay there until I collect you—if you know what is good for you.'

They stared at each other like enemies until Olivia's tight shoulders suddenly relaxed. It took an enormous effort, but she withdrew herself from all mental contact with him. If he thought she would allow him to goad and threaten her as a balm to his injured ego, then he was wrong. She was not about to give him the satisfaction.

'I'm not going to quarrel with you, Andreas. Let's just agree to keep out of each other's way, shall we? I only want to see Grandfather and then I'll go home and be out of your life.'

She turned back to the window, her face white and her hands trembling, but it was clear that he was not in any way upset.

'Avoiding each other will be rather difficult,' he remarked calmly. 'I shall be on the island for all the time you are there. I have plenty to do on Illyaros, but we shall be bound to meet and a modicum of civility will be necessary, if only not to upset Alex. Perhaps you could bring yourself to keep your childish tantrums under control and remember that I have no longer any reason to spoil and pamper you.'

'I was never spoiled!' she snapped, annoyed with herself as soon as the words were out. It seemed impossible to let anything go. She should just keep quiet, but everything Andreas said seemed to bring out the worst in her, to bring out the need to fight him.

'You were adored, worshipped. I should have put you over my knee and spanked you instead, then perhaps we would not be sitting here as strangers, tearing each other apart.'

'You certainly never adored me!' She clenched her hands and looked out of the window, hot waves of shame flooding over her. It sounded so much like a plea, as if she were begging to be assured that once she had meant something to him. He had loved her as a child, she could not deny that, but the feelings she had wanted from him later had never been there. She could hardly blame him for that. It was the deceit she blamed him for, the betrayal.

He did not even bother to answer and the grim silence continued as they sped across the city. Reluctantly, Olivia's mind turned back to Nicky and to the little scene she had had with Aunt Beth. She hated quarreling with her aunt, she would never forget the help she had given when things were at their blackest.

With no qualifications, no money and a baby on the way, she had been entirely dependent on Aunt Beth and had stayed in Scotland with her for those first few terrible months.

Andreas had opened a bank account for her and had later transferred it to London when she had moved, but she had never even called at the bank, although she supposed he was still paying money into it even now that they were divorced; money meant nothing to Andreas.

Peter had taken her on at the busy solicitors' office, with no qualifications whatever; those had been gained later at evening classes when Nicky was safely tucked up in bed and Aunt Beth was settled to look after him.

She had a measure of independence now that she had never had in her life. She had never felt the need to be independent with Andreas and he would never have allowed it, she had been under his shadow since childhood, it seemed.

It was Aunt Beth's disapproval that had forced the

quarrel. She had always sided with Andreas, had always felt that it was wrong, even wicked, to keep the birth of his son a secret, and she often gave voice to her resentment that Olivia should have to work so hard when Andreas could have kept her in luxury.

It was a great pull to go out every day and leave Nicky, not seeing him until the evenings, and she devoted every spare minute at the weekends to him, a fact that often brought friction between herself and Peter.

Aunt Beth's stubborn defence of Andreas had brought about the unusually sharp argument of the previous evening.

'It just hurts me to see you and Nicky separated. It hurt me when you divorced Andreas. It hurt him too, I expect.'

'He never contested it.' Olivia had turned away to avoid further harsh words, putting Nicky into his pyjamas and tickling him until he rolled about, squealing with laughter.

'He went mad when you left him. Day after day he pleaded with you when you were living with me, and you never even spoke to him—don't tell me he wasn't hurt. The terrible time you had with Nicky—Andreas should have been there, but you wouldn't let me send for him. Sometimes I've wished that I'd never taken any notice of you,' her aunt repeated doggedly.

'His pride suffered a severe jolt!' Olivia had snapped, losing patience. 'I'm the one that got away, Andreas doesn't like to lose his possessions. To be deserted and divorced was an unthinkable blow to his almighty arrogance. Don't class him with anyone you know—he's Greek. He doesn't react like an Englishman. Don't class him with Peter.'

'I don't!' her aunt had replied scornfully, and marched off to get supper.

'Anyway, there'll be no need for me to work when

Peter and I are married.' Olivia followed her, carrying Nicky on her hip, already regretting her outburst. 'Peter's not a millionaire, but he's a very successful solicitor. He'll be senior partner in five years when Neville Banks retires. We'll have a comfortable home.'

'If that's what you want,' her aunt replied tartly. 'At your age I should have thought you wanted love.'

'I love Peter.'

'Hmph!' Aunt Beth began to set the table with a certain angry vigour. 'Love was what you had with Andreas. Just to see you two together gave me a thrill—that's love.'

'And look where it got me!'

Olivia had put Nicky in his chair, pulling a plastic coverall over his pyjamas. She didn't like quarrels, and certainly not with her aunt, but more than that she didn't want to talk about Andreas. Love had turned to indifference after three years and Aunt Beth had been her sole support when things were at their blackest.

Oh, it was true, Andreas had followed her, begging her to go back to him until she had almost stopped believing the evidence of her own eyes, but he had tired of that quickly. One day he had not come round to her aunt's house in the quiet suburbs of Edinburgh, and when her aunt rang his hotel, even she had been shocked to find that he had simply gone, checked out and returned to Greece without a single word.

All hopes had died then and the only times she had heard from Andreas had been through his London lawyers. The only times she had seen him had been when the newspapers, in their endless pursuit of him, had found him in some nightclub, or holidaying on the yacht of one of his powerful friends.

Olivia came to the present with a start of surprise as Tomas slid the Mercedes silently into the parking area in front of the Meridien. So lost in her thoughts, her resentment, she had noticed little of the city they had passed through and her mind was still confused, madly fluctuating between the past and the present when Tomas deposited her luggage inside the luxurious suite that had been reserved for her, moving back outside to stand impassively by the lift as he waited for Andreas.

'You should be comfortable here.'

Andreas stood just inside the room and she wished Tomas had left the door open. There was suddenly a brooding darkness to his glance that alarmed her and quickened her heartbeats.

His eyes skimmed the elegance of the small sitting room. 'If you need anything, tell me when I call you later this afternoon.' Olivia did not answer and he looked at her in aggressive silence, his black brows drawn together in a scowl.

'Do you need any money?' Her green eyes met his coldly as he stared at her.

'No!' She was not going to be intimidated, even if it meant being rude.

'I'll put these in your bedroom.' He turned to the suitcases, but Olivia moved at the same time, her ungloved hand coming out to stop him. He was being polite and helpful, but to her he was treating her like a child, the way he had always treated her—besides, she wanted to get him out of the room, her reaction to him was alarming her.

'There's no need.' Their fingers met on the largest case, and suddenly, he froze. For a second she was mystified until her eyes followed his gaze—a gaze that was riveted on the diamond engagement ring she wore.

'What is this?'

He straightened, gripping her hand and looking ferociously into her startled face, the words driven out in an angry hiss between his clenched white teeth.

'My engagement ring.' She attempted to withdraw her hand, but it was impossible. 'You're hurting me, Andreas! Let me go!'

For one terrifying second, he looked angry enough to kill her. His dark eyes held hers in a glare that was almost corrosive, his colour fading until he was white to the lips.

'You dare to come back to me, wearing another man's ring?' He had stepped closer, gripping her arm, and she knew there was no escape from him.

'I haven't come back to you! I'm here only to see Grandfather. I'll never come back again!' Panic lent strength to her voice as he suddenly grasped her shoulders, pulling her against the hardness of his chest.

'My wife wears my rings and no others!' His eyes suddenly went to the smooth sweep of her hair and his hand gripped her shoulder more cruelly as his free hand went to the pins that kept her shining hairstyle in place.

'And get rid of these—I hate them, as you well know.' He began to move them, tossing them on to the carpet in spite of her struggles until her hair was loose and falling free around her shoulders.

'That's better. You will not put up barriers and disguises against me. Now we will dispense with this!' Andreas grasped her hand, wrenching the ring from her finger and throwing it into the farthest corner of the room.

Tears of rage and panic were streaming down Olivia's face as she fought to get away. She could not fight his strength, and frustration added speed to the flow of hot tears as she struggled madly, her hair falling around her face.

He shook her into silence and submission, his eyes burning with fury.

'Now, Olivia, you will stay here until I call for you. Do you hear me?'

'I hate you! You're an unspeakable pig! I hate you!' the words were choked from her as his hand moved into her long hair, his fingers winding themselves fast until her head was held at a rigid angle.

'Hate away, but obey me.' His voice was low and controlled, but there was danger in the dark eyes.

'You've no right to touch me! I'm not your wife any longer!' She was sobbing out the words, and his eyes narrowed at once.

'Nobody else has any right to touch you, and if anyone has, I'll kill them.' He pulled her face close to his, his teeth bared in a ferocious snarl. 'And don't keep telling me that you are not my wife! If you say it for much longer I will show you that you are, in no uncertain way.'

She thought he was going to kiss her and a wild mixture of fear and excitement raced through her at the prospect. He would hurt her, she knew. He had never been physically violent with her, had never shown her anything but gentleness, but this was Andreas as the world knew him. His temper was almost out of control and she waited for the savagery of his kiss.

It did not come, instead he relaxed the ferocity of his grip, his eyes losing some of the fierce anger as he read her expression.

'Now do as you are told,' he said more softly. 'Stay here and rest until I call for you.' His fingers in her hair seemed to have forgotten to pull so harshly. They were softly massaging the base of her neck where they had been so recently cruel.

'I hate you!' The thought of the excitement she had felt at the possibility of his kisses drove her on to defy him, but he only nodded grimly.

'I know. I can see that only too well.' He tipped her head up towards him. 'Even so, do not forget what I have said. You may hate me all you wish, but you—are—mine!'

Every word was driven out clearly as his hands tightened on her and then he let her go, striding from the room and closing the door quietly and firmly as if his demonic burst of anger and violence had never been.

Olivia sank on to the settee, her legs too weak to support her.

'Damn you, Andreas! Damn you for all the torment you've given me, for all the torment you'll give me until I'm safely out of your clutches.'

She struggled to her feet and walked to the far corner of the room, searching the carpet until she found her ring, pushing it back on to her trembling finger, her tears starting again. She would not leave it off. If he hoped that she would pretend to still be his wife so that his pride should not be shattered further, then he was mistaken.

She went back to the settee and lay down, putting her feet up. She was tired from the flight, from the small but real agony of parting with Nicky, but most of all she was exhausted by the short time she had spent with Andreas. Angry and bitter, very seriously worried, she was alarmed at the effect they had on each other.

There had always been a fierce physical attraction between them, ever since she had awakened to her feelings for him when she was seventeen. Any thoughts that they would meet as near relatives and continue politely like that for the whole of her stay could now be dismissed as ridiculous.

She realised with shame and fright that she had wanted him to kiss her, however ferociously, and she had seen for one brief second the flare of recognition and desire in his eyes. He might love another, might have loved another always, but when they were together everything between them seemed to leap towards each other with a sort of wild homing instinct.

They would fight every time they met unless she gave in to Andreas, and she would never do that. The situation was impossible.

CHAPTER TWO

IT had not always been like this. Olivia closed her aching eyes and remembered how she had first come to Greece when she was fourteen years old. Her grandfather had been in almost total control of the Skouradis business empire then and Andreas had been more free to enjoy himself. Time enough, her grandfather had said, for Andreas to devote himself entirely to the business when he was a few years older.

But at twenty-five, Andreas was already as astute as the old man and eager to take the reins in his strong hands. Sometimes it seemed that Alex Skouradis had some ulterior motive for keeping Andreas partially removed from the deeper affairs of the business when everyone knew that one day he would take over everything. For the moment, though, he had time to enjoy himself, time for Olivia.

He had always called her cousin, though in reality there was no relationship between them. Alex Skouradis had no sons, his children had both been girls, but the fact had never grieved him. Neither was he annoyed when his younger daughter married an Englishman and went to live in London.

They visited the island often and when Olivia was born, her grandfather doted on her. She was his first, and as things were to turn out, his only grandchild.

It was during this time that his older daughter married a Greek, a widower with a teenage son, and from that time, the future for Andreas was settled. Her father had apparently taken one look at him and declared him to be a Skouradis. His name was changed and he came to live on the island, Olivia's grandfather training him to run the business affairs, preparing him like a prince who would one day rule a kingdom.

Olivia barely remembered him. It was only when her parents died tragically in a car accident, and her grandfather summoned her to Greece, that her life became entangled with Andreas.

It was his comforting shoulder she cried on in the months following her parents' death. It was Andreas who drew her back into the laughter and happiness of simply being alive and in the sun.

He spoiled and pampered her, taking her with him wherever he went, even from the first, until he became her whole world. Together they sailed in the blue waters around Illyaros, swam in the warm sea, ran laughing across the sand, her long hair flying like a pennant behind her as he gave chase. If anyone thought it odd that he should be content with the company of a slender, leggy fourteen-year-old, they never said; Andreas even then was a dangerous and disquieting man, but never to Olivia.

Because her mother had been Greek, she had spoken the language since birth, and under the strict tuition of Andreas, she perfected it until she spoke her own language rarely, until she thought herself as Greek as Andreas, as Greek as her proud grandfather and the ever-present Tomas.

Old friends forgotten, she made new ones and delighted in the fact that as often as not she was called Olivia Skouradis instead of Olivia Page. She was where she belonged, where she had always been meant to be, in Greece with Andreas and in the sun, her waking hours filled with his laughter.

Olivia could not remember just when his protection became irksome to her, possibly when she was seventeen and rapidly approaching her eighteenth birthday. She no longer felt a child and resented the way any would-be boy-friend was scrupulously cut from her life. As soon as any boy-friend showed undue interest in her, she was hauled off by Andreas. He seemed to resent anyone who paid too much interest in her, although he himself often spent long days away from the island, no doubt with women—probably Leandi Kastakis, she thought irritably.

Still, trips to Athens and Crete, even trips to Italy were dangled before her like juicy carrots and she always gave in. Never able to refuse Andreas anything, never able to resist the desire to be with him. She went on these suddenly urgent trips knowing full well that when she returned the would-be boy-friend would have found another girl, or would mysteriously have stopped coming to Illyaros, for the island was strictly private, the fortress of the Skouradis family where visitors came by invitation only, another line of power that Andreas kept in his strong brown hands.

Pictures flashed in her mind. Cameos of pain that contained Andreas and herself. Memories of her growing awareness of him, a devastating physical attraction that he encouraged with amused indulgence until it grew into a love too strong to be denied, too powerful to be hidden. Now his guiding hands lingered on hers when he helped her, his dark eyes held hers for endless moments when they spoke. In the house on the cliff, his gaze seemed to follow her wherever she went until it was all too much for both of them.

They were sailing the *Anatoli* when he had first kissed her. Olivia was standing by the rail watching the island as they sailed nearer when suddenly he had put the boat on to automatic and was striding across to her, dark and vital, his tanned frame covered only in the white shorts he wore for sailing.

She found herself spun into his arms, her mouth captured in light-tasting kisses that enchanted and aroused her, until she sighed her delight against his mouth.

'It had to happen sooner or later,' he whispered against her lips, 'and I'm tired of waiting, my sweet Olivia.'

He threaded his fingers through her hair and trailed soft swift kisses over her flushed cheeks and the silky skin of her neck and shoulders until she clung to him trembling, a swift surge of fright adding excitement to the moment.

'I don't know what to do,' she whispered innocently, and he laughed delightedly.

'I should hope that you do not, *eros mou*! I've guarded you like a tiger. I would be most startled to find that you had somehow become experienced.' He kissed her blushing cheeks and held her tightly, his teeth nibbling at her tender earlobe. 'I will teach you, my darling, but not now. For now you will continue to be a good girl, though maybe I will not need to guard you so fiercely in the future, yes?'

With a few kisses he had banished her childhood for ever, but in its place came a sweet excitement and longing that Andreas fuelled quietly and carefully. The hand on her shoulder was now possessive, his eyes watched her with thrilling promise and the quick kisses he gave her were now placed warmly and secretly on her lips.

At the time she had fondly imagined that her grandfather knew nothing of this. He was behaving no differently, and if he noticed that Andreas was now no longer willing to be alone with her, he gave no sign. Nothing had been said about the future, only one thing was certain, she loved Andreas and he loved her, it was all she wanted.

The strident and insistent clamour of the telephone awoke Olivia from what must have been a very deep sleep, because she had the distinct impression that it had been ringing for some time.

For a second she was disorientated and then realised

that she had fallen asleep stretched out on the settee of the small sitting room of her suite. Dry-mouthed, her blouse damp and crumpled, she reluctantly hauled herself to her feet to stop the irritation of the continuous sound.

Her voice was still drowsy as she answered the phone, her mind not yet attuned to the present, and the voice in her ear came as a shock, an unwelcome intrusion when she was still vulnerable from the dreams that her earlier reflections had brought.

'Where the hell have you been?' It was Andreas at his worst. 'I thought I told you to stay in your suite? If I had imagined for one moment that you intended to disobey me, I would have brought you to the apartment and locked you in! Where have you been!'

'I've been here all the time.' Olivia was answering in the old submissive way, still dazed from her sleep, reacting to the authority of the man who had ruled her life for so long. He coaxed and she surrendered, he ordered and she obeyed. It had always been like that, and now he had caught her off guard.

'Don't add lying to your other recent accomplishments! I've been ringing for long enough to know that you've just this moment rushed in!' The harshness of his voice began to penetrate the woolliness of her sleepy mind and the new Olivia emerged.

'For your information, I've been asleep! I had every intention of going out, but sleep overtook me and thwarted my plans. I'm not answerable to you, now or ever. I'll do precisely as I like! Now say what you have to say or get off the line.'

There was a moment's silence which Olivia found particularly sweet. Rarely did Andreas stop when in full flow. Her fighting words had temporarily robbed him of speech.

'I want—I would like you to join me for dinner at seven-thirty.' By some miracle he had controlled that violent temper of his, and catching sight of her reflection in the mirror above the slender-legged wall table, Olivia offered herself a dignified bow of congratulation. 'I've booked a table at the Meridien to make it unnecessary for you to travel anywhere. I'll send a message to your room when I arrive—if that meets with your approval.'

His temper was evidently under a tight rein, there was not even the edge of sarcasm to his voice, and she had the odd impression that he was standing by the phone in the apartment, his face as solemn as a boy's.

'I have to dine. It may as well be with you. I was going to have something sent up to my room, but I can easily come down to the dining-room.'

She had no intention of being charming, or even courteous. He could be as solemn as he liked, there was no way that she was going to fall back under his spell, she was too hard for that now.

With a little imagination she could hear his blood boiling and she waited with interest for the explosion that would normally come after such terse, not to say rude remarks had been used to address him.

'Good. Thank you. Please do not come until you get my message. Perhaps—if you really wish to go shopping—I can spare Tomas to go with you in the morning. It is a little late now, but there will be time before we leave for Illyaros tomorrow. Until seven-thirty then, Olivia.'

The line went dead and Olivia found her lips trembling. He had no need to explode, he had put her firmly in her place by his charm, and she was left feeling rather small and cheap. His ever-present generosity had once again left her feeling just a simpering extension of his powerful personality.

She needed a long soak in a hot bath, she decided, surveying her decidedly tatty image in the mirror—but first, tea. She had to return to a more steady frame of mind before she met Andreas again, she had to shake off the lingering magic of her dreams of the afternoon. Being vulnerable was the last thing she needed to be when she met him for dinner.

She rang for refreshments, and before they arrived, had unpacked her dress for dinner, her travelling outfit for tomorrow and some casual wear for her morning's shopping expedition, because she had every intention of going.

Her skin had not wholly lost its tan, she conceded as later she leisurely dressed for dinner. As she had lived in the hot sun for years, there was none of the insipid whiteness of skin that she so disliked. The deep tan had faded to pale gold and although her face was a little pale, her health had returned after the shattering experience of her flight from Andreas and the difficult and pain-filled birth of his son.

The silken folds of the jade green dress whispered around her ankles, and suddenly she felt young again— carefree. The trauma of her separation from Andreas had robbed her of her youthful enchantment with life and she realised, with a feeling of guilt and disloyalty, that Peter had encouraged her into a rather staid frame of mind.

Even this dress, that she had bought for a dinner party that she had attended with him, had met with Peter's disapproval. Covering only one shoulder and clinging to her breasts, it was too daring, he thought. She had worn it with a lacy stole rather than offend his sensibilities.

She reached for the stole now, but cast it aside impatiently. Just for a while, she was her own mistress. The mirror revealed a different Olivia from either the lovesick girl who had run from a husband who had betrayed her, or the efficient secretary who helped to run a busy solicitor's office.

She gave a final smoothing flick to her upswept hair

and fixed the swinging jade pendants in her ears. The effect was decidedly Greek, she thought, like some acolyte in a temple. Her lips twitched in self-mockery at these fanciful thoughts as she turned to the telephone and her call to London.

Aunt Beth's first words were of Andreas, and Olivia had to stifle the annoyance that leapt instantly to the surface.

'How does he look, Olivia?'

'Fierce, arrogant, ruthless. In other words, much the same as usual. What did you expect?' It was difficult to keep the exasperation from her voice, and obviously she didn't succeed because Aunt Beth came back quickly with,

'He wasn't always like that. He's a real man, Olivia. How do you expect him to be when he hasn't seen you for all this time? He's not one to crawl on his knees.'

'I expect nothing from him, except to continue to stay out of my life,' Olivia assured her wearily. 'Is Nicky there?'

He was, and so for the next few minutes Olivia was able to forget all her problems as she listened to the little voice wrestling with the intricacies of the telephone and the few words he could command.

Her hand strayed to the phone again after the chattering little voice was silent. Should she ring Peter? He was expecting a call, she knew, but for the moment she was felt free, unwilling to surrender her new-found personality to the words of caution that she knew would be offered.

Besides, Aunt Beth had managed to annoy her. It sometimes seemed that the whole world was ranged on the side of Andreas and he needed no help at the best of times. She had the uneasy feeling that she needed the reassurance of her fiancé's voice before she faced Andreas—that thought was not welcome either.

She moved resolutely away from the temptation of

the phone and wandered through to the dressing-table in the bedroom to stroke a little *Ivoire* on her wrists and throat, surprised to find that her eyes were bright with anticipation as she waited for Andreas to send for her.

He did not send for her, he came himself, making no attempt to enter her suite as she opened the door, but standing relaxed and dangerous in the open doorway as she moved back into the room to collect her clutchbag.

In white dinner jacket and dark trousers, he looked as he looked in everything else, his superb clothes a thin disguise to temper down the ferocity of the man himself. What had once seemed to be sheer vitality now appeared to be uncivilised power, a tiger beneath a veil of urbanity.

He watched her through hooded eyes as she came towards him, his thick dark lashes casting shadows on his high cheekbones, his sensuous lips in a thin straight line. He looked more Greek than he had ever done before, and suddenly she saw him as he saw himself—a husband deserted and wronged—a man totally without pity—certain of his own rights and duties, with the righteous wrath, the violent anger of a Greek peasant whose life had not been touched by the standards of the twentieth century.

Olivia's face paled as a chill swept her spine and goose pimples rose on the backs of her arms. Circumstances had forced her to put her head into the tiger's cage and he would show no mercy.

A thin smile tilted his lips and his eyes opened fully to stare at her in frank appraisal, his insolent stare running over her and then returning to the proud fullness of her breasts. He seemed to have forgotten both the violent scene he had created when he had discovered that she was engaged and the sharp way she had spoken to him on the telephone.

'I ask myself if you are more beautiful than ever, or if you are too different to be the Olivia I remember.' He tilted his head on one side and smiled sardonically. 'What is it about you, Olivia, that's different? Experience?'

His thoughts were running in a dangerous direction and she tried to hide her blushes with anger. She was different, she was the mother of his child. Did it show so much?

'I had all the experience I'll ever need with you!' she rejoined tartly, but he laughed softly.

'Not nearly long enough of it, kitten. I did not have you long enough, it seems, to change you into a woman, and yet you have changed, so I ask myself, why?'

'Bitterness originally, and later, disgust.' Olivia picked up her door key and brushed past him, gasping as he clicked the door firmly shut behind her and then by some sleight of hand extracted her key and placed it in his pocket.

'Give me the key!' She faced him in the deserted corridor, her green eyes flashing with anger, her colour high as he watched her with mocking dark eyes.

'We will see,' he said calmly. 'I am wondering whether or not to take you to the apartment after all. You would feel more at home there and less agitated.'

Olivia faced him silently, her colour flaring and her hand held stiffly in front of her, palm up.

'The key!' She did not move, her words gritted out between clenched teeth, and suddenly he laughed, dropping the key into her outstretched hand.

'Do not distress yourself, Olivia,' he grated harshly. 'My evening is arranged and my after-dinner plans do not include you.'

The erratic beating of her heart began to subside as he escorted her to the lift and then out into the foyer, but she had seen the devil in those eyes. She knew that this goading would continue for as long as it amused him, regardless of her grandfather's health. Suddenly she was relieved that soon she would have the reassuring presence of Peter to lean on. Her fingers sought the security of her engagement ring. He had noticed that she had replaced it on her finger, but he had said nothing. He would change his tactics with the same bewildering speed that he dealt with everything else, but she would soon be away from him.

She was calm again and wondered how she could have been so foolish as to not to wish to ring Peter, so foolish as to imagine that dinner with Andreas could be anything but fraught with unpleasantness. It was an embarrassment to remember how her heart had quickened when he had knocked on her door a few minutes ago. Any disgust she felt was towards herself.

'You would like a drink before dinner, Olivia?' He led her into the cocktail bar and his appearance was signalled around the room, like visiting royalty, she thought with annoyance. 'What do you drink now that you are grown up?'

'Dry sherry.' She was not going to rise to the bait. She had his measure now and nothing would unsettle her. All she had to do was last out until Peter came and they could leave the island together.

'You remember Leandi, I expect?'

The deep sardonic voice cut into her thoughts and Olivia raised shocked eyes to meet the dark triumphant gaze of Leandi Kastakis. Her hair was still the same—thick, glossy, black, pulled back and looped around her ears, her dark-skinned face flawless, her make-up immaculate. She appeared to have been poured into the red gown she wore and to Olivia's startled eyes, she looked as if she would at any time overflow from the top of it.

Suddenly, Olivia felt defeated. There was no limit to Andreas' cruelty. To bring the woman who was his mistress here, on her own first evening back in Greece, was the harshest blow he could have dealt her. At the side of Leandi, her own attempts at maturity and sophistication seemed pointless. The Greek woman was blatantly sexual, her predatory, red-nailed hand already reaching out to Andreas, pawing at the sleeve of his white jacket.

'Olivia! How nice!' She turned pouting red lips to Andreas. 'Darling, I hope you don't mind, but I thought it so cruel for Olivia to dine with just the two of us, so I've brought Takis to join us.'

Leandi urged forward the man who had been just behind her, and Olivia found herself looking into two eyes that she had never stopped disliking.

'You remember my brother Takis, Olivia? I don't actually recall if you ever met him when you were married to Andreas, but you can make up for it now, he always admired you from afar.'

'Only because I was not allowed to admire you from close up.' The dark eyes gleamed with speculation as the man with the striking good looks of his sister took Olivia's hand and raised it to his lips.

No, she had not met Takis after her marriage to Andreas, and very little before that. Andreas had dealt with him speedily as soon as he had seen the effect that Olivia had on him. She risked a sideways glance at Andreas and her spirits rose, threatening to bubble over. He was furiously angry, stiff with rage and barely in control of himself. He too had noticed the look in the eyes of Leandi's brother and he liked it no more now than he had done when Olivia was seventeen.

He took her arm in a punishing grip, ignoring the drinks and striding forward, telling them tightly that their table was ready.

The biter bit! Olivia had to struggle to hide her laughter as they followed the head waiter to their table. What had been meant as a cruel trick had backfired on Andreas and the swift stab of feeling, frighteningly akin to jealousy, that she had experienced at the sight of

Leandi, still clearly the mistress of Andreas, dissolved as she realised that he too felt more deeply than she had thought.

His idea of an evening's entertainment at her expense was now foiled completely and she would not have liked to be in Leandi's shoes when she had to face him later alone. She had brought Takis and had referred to Olivia's marriage as being most definitely in the past. What other crimes she would commit during the evening Olivia did not know, but she anticipated them with a certain amount of glee.

It was Andreas who settled her into her chair and fussed quietly until she was comfortable, leaving Leandi to her brother. It was Andreas too who ordered for her when she indicated with a careless wave of her hand that she was not concerned with food. He chose all the things that had once been her favourites and her earlier confidence returned when she saw that neither this, nor his angry reception of her brother, had been lost on Leandi.

Sitting at a round table, Olivia would have not thought it possible for one person of a party of four to indicate that she was alone with one of the party, but Leandi managed it, ignoring Olivia and Takis and pouring attention upon Andreas in a sultry stream of nuances and syrupy glances that sickened Olivia and embarrassed Takis as they ate their meal.

Andreas said very little, his good humour by no means restored, and finally Takis said with an air almost of desperation,

'I see that you are engaged, Olivia.' It was rather like dropping a pebble into a pool and finding that it was, after all, a boulder. It captured Leandi's attention and drew the cold ferocity of Andreas towards the unfortunate Takis.

'Yes.' Olivia decided to enjoy the evening. Andreas could hardly pretend that she was his wife here, amongst people who knew with utmost certainty that she was not. 'I'm getting married in three months. Peter will be joining me in a few days time and we'll go back to London together.'

Andreas was a black presence at the table, his lean tautly muscled frame poised on the brink of violence. They all felt it, and Leandi held her tongue. Olivia realised that even as his mistress she was allowed no leeway, must bow to the power and anger of Andreas like everyone else. She realised with great satisfaction that she was the only one at the table who did not fear him.

Her smile, as Takis hastily asked her to dance, was full of brilliance that took in the wary face of Leandi and the imperious anger of Andreas. So long as Nicky was safe, she cared for nothing.

'I think you are more beautiful than ever, Olivia.' They had already circled the floor once before Takis spoke and Olivia was hard pressed to keep the smile on her face. Apart from his resemblance to his sister, she didn't like the way he spoke to her nor the way he looked at her. It was with a slight shiver of revulsion she realised that he would very much like to paw her, if he had dared. It was not her withdrawn, icy smile that held him off either, it was fear of Andreas, she had no doubt about that.

She had never had to put up with this sort of attention in her life. Protected by Andreas, she had been cosseted against the manner that she sensed under the well-oiled smile of Takis. Her life since then had been sheltered too, both by the fact that she had a son to raise and by the fact that Peter's acquaintances were definitely not of the flirtatious variety.

'I hope that my remarks at the table do not bring trouble down on your beautiful head.'

'Trouble? I don't understand.' She did, but there was

no way that Takis was going to be allowed to carry tales back to his sister.

'Trouble in the form of Andreas.' His eyes told her that he knew of her small deception. 'He can be extremely unnerving when that anger is upon him, and he did not like the mention of your fiancé.'

'I'm divorced from Andreas. His wishes no longer concern me.' Olivia looked around the room and looked away quickly as she found Andreas watching her, his dark eyes following their progress.

'He is clever and ruthless, an empire builder in the modern idiom, but in many ways he is very old-fashioned. I have heard it said that he still considers you to be his wife.'

Olivia looked at him coldly, tired now of the games and annoyed at his intrusion into her private life.

'Andreas may think whatever he wishes. We lead separate lives.' She was quite capable of keeping him in his place and she sensed that as the dance ended, he was rather relieved to take her back to the table.

'If that is so, then perhaps I can see you while you are here?' The practised charm was out again, the smile intimate and insinuating. 'May I call to see you tomorrow?'

'I think not. Tomorrow I'm going out to Illyaros with Andreas. Of course you could see me there, if you're one of the chosen few who are allowed to land on the island.'

'I think you know that I am not, Olivia. You tease me. It is exhilarating, but frustrating.'

His last words were clearly audible to the two at the table and Andreas was on his feet before she had time to sit.

'Dance with me.'

'Oh, I think . . .'

'Come.' He took her arm and once again she found herself circling the floor.

He had shaken her and hurt her with the cruelty of his grip earlier in the day, but it was a long time since those arms had really held her. She could feel the seething anger within him and said nothing about the punishing grip of his hands on her waist, but simply waited for the words she knew would explode from him.

'You will keep away from Kastakis!' His voice was a threatening thunder close to her ear. To any onlooker they appeared to be dancing in close embrace, an intimacy about them that spoke of lovers, but Olivia was aware that his arms were a prison until he chose to release her.

'I fully intend to keep away from him, and from his sister too. I imagine that the same poison runs in both their veins.'

Whether he had expected her to tease him with the charms of the good-looking Takis or not she did not know, but her words seemed to surprise him. He drew back and looked down at her averted face, his dark eyes running over its creamy perfection.

'You've grown a little poisonous yourself, Olivia,' he said softly.

'I wonder why?' she exclaimed tartly, looking up into his cynical face. 'I expect it's called maturity. You did say that I'd grown up, didn't you, Andreas?'

His face darkened and he pulled her back close to him with a muttered imprecation. 'You are very different. More changed than I expected. There is something that I can't quite put my finger on—no doubt it will come to me.'

Olivia tried not to stiffen. She hoped that it would not come to him. Motherhood changed women more than anything else, except perhaps love. If Andreas suspected that some great change had taken place, he would probe and dig until he found out. She held her tongue, determined not to show anything else of her new character, fear rising in her throat as he wove skilfully through the other dancers on the crowded floor.

After a while, he relaxed, she felt it run through him almost like a sigh and his hands lost their cruel grip. They had danced like this so often, it was easy to be seduced into dreaming that the past had never happened, that there was still only Andreas in her life, his laughter, her sunshine.

'Why do I worry about Kastakis?' His breath was warm on her forehead, stirring her hair, and she fought down the old excitement. 'Tomorrow we go to Illyaros and he knows that he is not welcome there. His attempts at that began and ended when you were seventeen. He was an ardent admirer, or so he told me at the time, before I threw him off the island.'

Olivia stared at him in astonishment. She had not known that.

'A little late for him now, don't you think? Peter will be here in a couple of days, or even sooner.'

'And you expect me to allow him access to my island? The chance to be with my wife? You expect that—of me?' He looked almost surprised that she should so misread his character that she had invited another man to her grandfather's home.

'If not, then I leave.' Her flat statement caused the beautiful dark eyes to narrow dangerously, but he obviously did not want an argument here.

'What is he like—this fiancé?' His slow drawl warned her that he had a grip on himself, and she tensed to meet the sarcasm.

'Perfectly ordinary. Tall, fair, a solicitor.' She avoided the penetration of his eyes and glanced brightly round the room.

'Does he think that you are only worth this trinket?' He fingered her ring and when she struggled, his hand tightened cruelly, pressing the ring into the softness of her fingers. 'Why did you not take the beautiful emerald with you, that I bought to match your eyes?'

'I no longer considered it to be of value!' The pressure of his fingers was bringing tears of pain to her eyes and he relaxed his grip, his black brows drawn together in a scowl.

'You could have sold it and lived for three years on the proceeds. As you would not touch the money that I placed in the account I opened for you, at least you could have sold your ring, then you would not have been reduced to working for a living.'

'How do you know I work?' For a minute her heart almost stopped. If he knew that, what else did he know?

'My London office have kept a loose rein on you. How else do you think that Alex could have sent you a cable? You have never had the courtesy to write to him.'

She was thankful now of the precautions she had taken with Nicky. The seemingly stupid steps she had taken to cover up the fact that a child was living in the flat with herself and Aunt Beth. How long could she keep this up?

'Why did you drive yourself to working so hard, when I could have kept you in luxury, Olivia?'

'You work hard, as I remember,' she taunted.

'But my wife does not!' He regarded her narrowly. 'Or are you saving my money to use as a dowry for this Englishman?'

'He wants nothing of yours!' Olivia snapped.

'On the contrary—he wants my wife. My greatest possession.' The words were quiet, but held a menace greater than anything he had yet said. She would have pulled away from him—stormed off to her room, but he held her implacably, placing her hands on his hard, muscled chest, trapping them there, his arms tightly around her slender waist.

'I'm not your wife! Can't you get that fixed into your

head?' It was too much of a strain to look up at his superior height and her savage remarks were addressed to the middle button of his shirt.

'We have discussed this already and I have explained that I am Greek,' he said with infuriating calm.

'And another thing,' she stormed. 'I'm not your possession!'

One powerful finger tipped her face towards his.

'No?' His intent night-black gaze held hers. 'You were always my possession Olivia, from the first moment I saw you as a child. Your defection has not altered my way of thinking.'

'In the eyes of the law, I'm a single woman.' Her voice sounded desperate, even to her own ears, and Andreas smiled slowly.

'And in my arms, you are my wife. Tomorrow we go to Illyaros—home. There, I am the law. You will be made to realise how foolish you are.'

She raised her head in shocked surprise and was instantly pinned by the glittering jet of his arrogant gaze.

'Then I'll not go to Illyaros. I'll leave Greece tomorrow. I'll not be a prisoner!'

'You have been a prisoner since you landed on Greek soil, Olivia,' he purred softly. 'I doubt if you could simply leave without my permission. I have too many friends in high places.'

'I'll go to the British Embassy!'

'You think that you will get there? Even if you escape me, this time I shall follow you and see exactly what you are up to. I didn't realise that you were engaged, Olivia, that a secret love life was being lived out in that sordid little solicitors' office, that you planned to commit bigamy. If I had, I would have been in London long ago to get you.'

The trump card. If he came to London, he would find Nicky. She was more of a prisoner than he realised, and her head bowed in defeat.

'Why are you doing this, Andreas? You don't care about me, you never did.'

'You say that—to me?' One hand left her waist to slide behind her head, his thumb tipping her face up until she was forced to meet the shuttered stillness of his eyes. 'You think that I have never cared for you? You have a very weak memory, Olivia. *Theos!* You were barely sixteen when I first wanted you.'

'Wanting isn't loving, Andreas!' It was increasingly hard to glare into those eyes when everything about him reminded her of her past happiness.

'No, it is not. I wonder if you ever knew the difference.' He looked at her in angry frustration for a moment and then released her face, tightening his hands on her waist again.

'Oh, be quiet, Olivia. You are more tiring than a day's work.' He sank into sombre silence and Olivia's mind worked frantically. Some way she had to get the better of him, but how? He would take Nicky and she would never see him again unless she gave in and stayed with Andreas, a balm for his injured pride, so that everyone would know that his wife had realised her foolishness, her wickedness, and returned. So that Andreas could go on as before, loving Leandi, living his own private life.

She wished now that she had called Peter. As soon as she got back to her room she would call him. The thought put some colour back into her face, and seeing it, Andreas laughed softly.

'Ah! You have a plan? You are intriguing, Olivia, there is more to you now than meets the eye, though what meets the eye is delightful enough.'

She raised her head and gasped at the expression in his eyes.

'You're worth waiting for, Olivia—but not for much longer.'

She spun away from him then, gathering her bag and

walking out of the room, uncaring that interested eyes followed her. Her legs were unsteady, her heart hammering wildly, knowing that Leandi and Takis watched her hot shame, the deep flush that would not leave her face.

Let them think what they liked, at least she had the satisfaction of seeing the wild look of jealousy on Leandi's face. Brushing past Andreas without looking at him, she made for the lift, wishing with all her heart she had refused to see her grandfather and was still in the flat with Nicky and Aunt Beth.

He caught her as the lift door opened, stepping in with her and punching the button for her floor.

'Twice you've run out on me in public!' he snarled. 'Do it again, Olivia, and I won't be responsible for what happens!'

'Just leave me alone!' Her eyes were filled with humiliation and hatred. 'I hate you Andreas! I don't ever want to speak to you again. When we get to the island I hope you'll realise that you're nothing to me and keep out of my way. I won't be used as a sop to your injured pride.'

'Ah! So you have decided to stay after all. Very wise. It saves a lot of unseemly disturbance. We have had enough of that, I think.'

'Disturbance!' Her voice was shrill with anger. 'You expect no disturbance when you invite your ex-wife and your mistress to dinner at the same time? Is that what Greeks call civilised behaviour?'

'You were proud to be Greek once—to be married to a Greek.'

'As you pointed out, so truthfully, I was a child then.'

She stormed out of the lift as it stopped and would have run to her room had he not prevented her, his hand hard on her upper arm.

'Calm down, Olivia. Nothing is going to happen to you. I had a vicious wish to see you suffer, but I think you have been frightened enough. You are quite safe from me.' He gripped her chin, turning her face abruptly to his. 'You say you hate me. Can you imagine then how much I hate you, Olivia? I would not step into hell twice for any woman, and you are not a woman, you are still, deep down, the child I spoiled and pampered until she cared for nothing and no one but herself.'

'It's not true!' Her agonised rejection left him unmoved.

'Not true? How many times did you write to your grandfather? Did his love fail to satisfy you too? Would you have remarried without telling him, an old man who has loved you all your life? Oh yes, it is true, Olivia. You care for yourself alone. I hope that this fiancé realises this.'

She was speechless at the depth of dislike that flared in his eyes. She could only stare, utterly defeated, as he watched her stonily, only his eyes alive, alive with a feeling she had never thought to see in Andreas.

She could give no explanation. How could she? What would he say if she said, I couldn't risk anyone finding out about my son, our son? Even her love for her grandfather was pushed to the back when the necessity to protect and keep Nicky was paramount.

To keep him. Was that selfish? Spoiled and pampered? How would Andreas look if he knew that she was jealously guarding from him the son that he did not even know he had?

'Tomorrow, Tomas will collect you and take you on this shopping expedition that you are so set on. I know your self-indulgent ways too well not to realise that you will sneak off by yourself and walk into danger if I forbid you to go, therefore Tomas will escort you. You had better be ready on time, he is an early riser.'

She could only nod in silence, unable to take her eyes from his forbidding face. Suddenly he seemed much older than his thirty-three years, and for the first time she saw the cares of the empire he ran written across is face. If things had been different she would have been sharing those worries, ironing out those lines of strain.

She turned from him and stumbled to her room, locking the door and leaning against its cool hard surface, her clenched fist held tightly against her mouth until she heard his steps move from the door.

Then the dam of her misery broke and she slid to the floor, her sobs as heartfelt and childlike as Nicky's. Was she all that Andreas had said? What was wrong with her that he could still devastate her like this? Could wrench her heart even now because he looked tired, careworn.

She had her own future to defend. Once again she had seen Leandi with her own eyes, clearly still his mistress, still the one he loved.

She struggled to her feet, slipping out of her dress and creaming her face from sheer force of habit. Her nightdress was cool and comforting to her skin and for a long time she sat on the edge of the bed, her eyes staring blindly at her lifeless hands.

All he had said had been intended to alarm her, to punish her, to rob her of her new-found confidence. There had been no mistaking the hatred on his face, and she shuddered to think of the hatred she would see there if ever he found out about Nicky.

There was a feeling of sheer panic inside her because in the course of one day he had turned her safe little world upside down. She felt threatened by having walked into the trap of all that was Greece and the power that Andreas held there. Threatened also by her swift stab of jealousy at the sight of Leandi and her wave of emotion at the lines of strain on his face. She would never be safe from Andreas unless she was miles away from him. In one day he had opened old wounds, weakened her resolve and left her on the edge of despair.

She got up and walked to the telephone. It was late, but Peter would understand. She had to speak to him now, to cling to the safety he offered. Everything depended on his help.

CHAPTER THREE

NEXT morning, Olivia awoke with a feeling of heaviness
and desperation. For the first time in her life she felt
trapped. She had run from trouble before, escaping
from the pain she had felt when Andreas had betrayed
her. There had been no escape really, but at least she
had been free to run. Now, there was nowhere to run.

If she left, Andreas would follow, and Nicky could
not be hidden from him. To stay would bring conflict,
every day a nightmare as she faced his hatred. For the
first time, she felt that no one would help her. Peter had
been adamant—the Markington case could not be left.

In fairness to him she had to admit that she had not
told him the whole truth. She had begged him to come
at once, but had given no clear reason. How could she?
She was not even sure herself where her biggest fears
lay. There was nothing that Peter could do if Andreas
decided to follow her to London. She was on her own
for the first time ever, her wits against those of
Andreas, her strength of will against his, she would not
have liked to place a bet on her chances of winning
against him.

Tomas was at the door by nine o'clock and met her
teasing with his usual wide grin.

'I thought you were an early riser, Tomas. Andreas
warned me to be ready in good time and I've been hanging
around for ages. What time do you call this, then?'

'I call it nine o'clock, Kyria Skouradis, and before
you berate me too much, perhaps I had better tell you
that Andreas asked me not to call too early. He said
that you had been upset last night and that a sleep in
would do you good.'

'Oh.' Olivia did not know what to say to this piece of information. Andreas had showed no sign of caring about her state of health last night. She collected her shoulder bag, making a determined effort to be natural with Tomas. She had always been fond of him. He was like a big dog, faithful to those he loved, ferocious with enemies.

'I suppose I was tired,' she said brightly, stepping out into the corridor.

'I expect so, Kyria Skouradis.' His face gave nothing away and after a quick glance, she let the matter drop.

'It is very good to have you back, Kyria Skouradis,' he said quietly as they stepped into the hot street, and she linked her arm with his, swinging along with him as she had done since childhood, to his obvious surprise and delight.

'I'm not that any more, Tomas,' she corrected gently. 'Call me what you've called me ever since you've known me.'

'Very well, Despinis Olivia. To spoil this day with quarrels would be a crime.' He looked uneasy, but with a determined effort on both sides, they enjoyed the morning, and a little of the dread of her coming meeting with Andreas at lunch lifted as they spent the morning wandering around the shops.

She bought small gifts for her grandfather and Sophia, who had served the Skouradis family for so long that to them she was Aunt Sophia. Any gift for Nicky would have to wait, she decided. Tomas determinedly stuck to her side and she refused to resort to subterfuge to explain why she was buying gifts for a child.

She deliberately let her mind move back in time, let her vivid imagination take her back into the happiness of days when life had been good, but life had been Andreas, and his dark scowls at lunch showed her only too clearly that his words of last night had not been said lightly.

He avoided her gaze, not with any deliberate effort, but with an ease that showed his thoughts were so far away that she might as well not have existed.

Well, that was what she wanted, wasn't it? She told herself firmly that it was, that his indifference was what she had hoped for from the first. He had finished playing his cruel games, had tired even of looking at her. There was safety in that, and she would settle for safety any day. Soon, she would be back with Nicky and she would never see Andreas again. His threats to keep her here had been only another means of playing with her mind, another cruel joke. He would be glad to see the last of her.

The sleek white boat was ready as they came to the harbour, and Olivia saw with a lifting of spirits that it was the same, the *Anatoli*—*Sunrise*—where she had spent so many happy days with Andreas. He usually handled the boat alone, but now he turned to Tomas as they left the harbour and indicated the wheel.

'You will take us, Tomas.' It was not a request, and Tomas silently took over as Andreas leaned against the rail, looking out to sea, his eyes narrowed against the wind, his hair lifting in the old familiar curl.

Olivia felt her heart contract with pain and she turned away to look in the opposite direction. There would be time enough to face the same way again when Illyaros came in sight.

There was no sound except the humming of the powerful engines, the slap of water against the side of the boat, and the occasional sound of a screaming gull as it swept in greedy exploration over the boat.

She did not hear Andreas approach, the sound of the boat had drowned his steps across the deck, and her memories of the past were still on her face as she felt his hands on her shoulders.

He turned her and for a second looked down at her, his eyes questioning as they read her expression, his dark gaze lingering on her lips.

'Your mouth is still too wide, still too beautiful,' he observed softly, turning her away before she could think of an answer and pointing out across the blue, sparkling water.

'Look—Illyaros. We are almost home, Olivia.'

Home. Yes, it was that. Her heart admitted it as she saw again the golden cliffs that fell sheer to the sea, the sundrenched, thickly wooded hills outlined against a clear blue sky.

The brightly painted dome of the little church where she had been married to Andreas rose above the whitewashed houses of the pretty village that nestled in the pine woods, and in her mind's eye she could see the narrowed winding lanes between the flowered balconies.

The stronghold of the Skouradis family was not a deserted island. A good water supply made it an ideal place to live and the few farmers and fishermen who made up the population of Illyaros were as devoted to Andreas as they had been to her grandfather.

Nothing happened on the island that was not reported to the family. In bad times, the wealth of the Skouradis family was used to aid the villagers, and in good times, their rising fortunes were attributed to the patronage of Andreas and her grandfather.

One word from the old mansion that stood proudly above the next headland was law to the villagers of Illyaros, and Olivia realised with a thrill of fear that she would soon be in a fortress, a beautiful island that would be heaven or hell, depending on the whim of Andreas.

Certainly, if she decided to leave without his permission, there would be no one on the island, including Tomas, who would be prepared to help her. She had been an object of affection to them all, but when she had left Andreas, she had forfeited all their respect. She did not need anyone to tell her that.

To them she was still Madame Skouradis, a wilful girl who had deserted her Greek husband. She could hope for no aid, and only the presence of Andreas and the name of her husband would protect her from their scorn.

She looked up to find Andreas watching her closely. He had released her shoulders and moved to the rail to stand with his back to the sea and he was observing every expression that crossed her face.

'You return with mixed feelings,' he said astutely. 'Do you think you will be able to hate so completely when the past is all around you?' His dark eyes were narrowed and intent.

'None of us can escape from the past,' Olivia said softly. 'It makes us what we are.'

'I fail to see how the past that we had could have made you suspicious and unsure,' he remarked bitterly. 'You walked as a goddess on this island, proud as Athene, every step you took taken in the certain knowledge that you were prized above all else, above all women.'

'Words, Andreas! Fancy, poetic Greek words! Reality beats words every time.'

'That I can vouch for, and I promise you reality this time,' he said with deadly quiet. 'I would say with utmost certainty that your childhood is over.'

'It was over a long time ago,' she retorted, her eyes cold and green. 'There's nothing like a shock for jolting the system.' She turned her back, unwilling to continue this bickering. There had been a tenderness in his arm as he had turned her to the island, now there was a black emptiness in his stare.

She was to be spared the walk through the village from the main harbour, she saw, as the *Anatoli's* gleaming prow veered away to the right and made for the tiny private landing stage that nestled beneath the golden cliff that was topped by the Skouradis house.

Andreas had given no order and she felt a surge of gratitude towards Tomas, until she realised that Andreas would no more like to run the gauntlet of those scornful eyes than she would herself. A man was less than successful who could not keep his wife in order, and it dawned on her for the first time just how much pity and quiet astonishment must have been directed at Andreas during the three years of her absence.

She was not surprised at his hatred. He seemed to imagine that he could live by a different set of rules from other people. That he had betrayed her, that he had kept Leandi as his mistress, was as nothing to him compared with her flight from him. He had married her to satisfy her grandfather and to secure the future of the Skouradis empire and he was prepared to stick to that, in his own way.

The memory of the day she had burst into his office and found Leandi in his arms swamped all other thoughts and stilled her smile of pleasure at her homecoming. This was not her home. This was the seat of power of a tyrant who would do as he pleased, whatever hurt it brought to others.

By the time the boat was berthed by the neat steps that led to the cliff top, her bitterness was fully returned, and it was with cold eyes and a grim face that she stepped ashore, her hand snatched from the helping fingers of Andreas as soon as her feet touched the landing stage.

She walked off alone as the two men made fast the boat and by the time they were ready, her slim, lonely figure was halfway up the wide deep steps of the cliff. She would face what had to be faced and then leave Illyaros with Peter. To imagine any lingering love for Andreas was as ridiculous as her marriage had been, the

fairytale daydreams of a lovesick girl. To imagine that
he intended to keep her here was an idea that could be
dismissed now. He had finished playing his games. He
would be glad to see her go.

It was Sophia who met her at the door, her lined
brown face a picture of uncertainty. For a second she
hovered between affection and reproof, her hands
clenched at her sides as she looked at Olivia with eyes
filled with the brightness of tears.

'Olivia!' She took a hesitant step forward and then
affection won as with a rush she gathered the slender
figure in her arms. '*Kalimera*, child, you have brought
back the sunlight!'

'Tia Sophia,' Olivia was on the edge of tears herself
as she realised the pain that her absence must have
brought to this kindly woman who had helped to raise
her. Sophia's whole life had been one of devotion to the
family, she had thought of Olivia's mother as her own
daughter and had filled the gap of her death with an
outpouring of love on to Olivia.

Even to her, though, Andreas was never wrong, and
she extricated herself from the enfolding arms with a
deep sigh. Her grandfather had to be faced now, and
she would not be surprised at anything that he said to
her. He had not begged her to come back to Illyaros.
His cable had been an order, an order which she had
obeyed. He was ill, but he was clearly still the fierce
domineering man who had ordered her marriage to
Andreas.

'Where is he?' She dabbed at her eyes with her
handkerchief and turned a wary smile on Sophia. 'I
think I should see him at once, unless he's resting.'

'Resting? That one?' Sophia assumed her usual role
of scornful contempt. 'To get him to rest is
impossible. Now that he is recovering he is as bad as
ever, interfering in everything. You will find him in
his room. That is the only concession he makes to

age and illness, he keeps to his room, but one of these days he will drive that chair of his off the balcony while he is peering down and minding everyone's business!'

Olivia's muscles stiffened in shock.

'He's in a wheelchair?'

'Why, yes. Did no one think to tell you, child?' Sophia's arm came round her protectively. 'Don't worry, he is recovering. You go up and burst in on him.' She smiled wickedly. 'The shock will do him good, although I should think that he has probably been watching the *Anatoli* put in, through those binoculars of his. Better that you go now before he begins to roar for your presence. I will make you a drink. Tea, eh? You will have got back into your old habit of tea-drinking.'

Olivia nodded and sped across the hall, climbing the old polished staircase and seeing with surprise that everything was still the same. The same deep red carpet on the stairs, the same polished tables in the wide hall, the same bowls to hold the displays of flowers. It seemed so long ago, and yet it was only three years. Why should she have expected change? Her grandfather liked things as they had always been, and whenever anything wore out he would have it replaced with an exact copy as long as he lived.

She hesitated outside his door, her hand on the gleaming brass of the knob, fearful of the meeting, yet wanting to see him with an urgency that surprised her. She drew a deep breath and opened the door, steeling herself for reproof.

There was none, though. He was sitting in a wheelchair facing the door, his strong craggy face pale and drawn, but still the same in other ways, the same aura of power, the same steely-eyed determination on his face. He liked his own way and saw to it that he got it. He had abdicated his position as head of the business, but he would never fully relinquish the power, he enjoyed it too much.

'Grandfather!' Olivia ran across the room, falling to her knees beside the chair and felt the years slip away as she was enclosed in a bear-hug by arms that still held the same strength that had greeted her when she had run to his protection at fourteen.

'There, child!' He held her away and looked closely at her tear-stained face. 'What did you expect? That the old lion would be in bed in a white nightcap? Now that you're here I shall have reason to get about more. I'll be down those stairs in a week.'

She could hardly believe that she was to escape a scolding, that he would not berate her for her desertion of Andreas and himself, but he seemed in no mood to take her to task, and she was relieved. The meeting was filled with emotion as it was, and she could well do without the trauma of facing his anger.

'Fetch that stool, Olivia, and sit where I can have you close.' She pulled up the tapestry-covered footstool and settled herself at his feet. So many times she had sat on that stool when she was a child as she had leaned against his armchair and listened hungrily to the tales and legends of Greece that he had filled her mind with when she had first come.

Andreas had laughingly said that he made many of the legends up as he went along and had advised her to check them with him before taking them too much to heart, but she had been enthralled to sit and listen to her grandfather as she sat now.

'Can't you walk, Grandfather?' she asked in a low voice.

'A little, a little,' he growled, 'but you know what Sophia is like. I am a prisoner in my own house, slowly growing old.'

Olivia hid a smile. She had heard this before, and though he looked ill, she had no doubt that he would recover. The old wheedling tones were there, a tone he reserved for times when orders would not succeed. 'Now you are here, child, I shall get well. Things will be back as they used to be and there will be laughter in the house again. You used to laugh such a lot. I have missed it. You were always that little bit impudent, even with Andreas.'

'I can't stay too long, Grandfather.' Better to let him know right away that no amount of pleading would keep her here. 'If it's all right with you, my fiancé will come out to join me in two days. We'll be able to go back to London together.'

His sharp intake of breath showed her that he had not been prepared for this blow, and she kept silent, wondering how he would take it.

'Your fiancé. What does Andreas say about this? Have you acquainted him with the fact that you intend to marry again?'

'Yes, he knows.' It was difficult to face the old man, but she made herself do it, and his gaze was sad rather than angry.

'You are married to Andreas, child. Nothing can alter that. He will never allow someone to take what is his, he is too much like me to permit such a thing— besides, he is Greek.'

Olivia felt a quick burst of anger at the oft-repeated, proud assertion, and her face coloured with temper.

'Greek enough to have a mistress! You know why I left Andreas, Grandfather, and why I divorced him. It just didn't work out as you hoped, and I intend to get some happiness in my life. What Andreas thinks is nothing to me any more. Unless you forbid it, Peter will join me. I want you to meet him. I've no quarrel with you, Grandfather.'

'Only with Andreas? And you think you can find happiness away from him?' He looked at her thoughtfully and then nodded his head. 'Yes, we should all meet your fiancé—let him come.'

There was a look in his eyes that Olivia would have hoped not to see. His cunning, as Andreas had said, was still very much intact, and she smiled with a certain amount of misgiving. Still, what could go wrong? She was engaged, her marriage only three months away. Neither her grandfather nor Andreas could do a thing about it and she would refuse to listen to the uneasy thoughts that swept through her mind, the quick stabs of pain that pierced her body when Andreas was near. It was over, and they were both glad really. It was only pride that kept Andreas from admitting it and treating her like a cousin again, she had seen the odd burst of affection in his face. She had seen the swift rise of desire too, but she pushed that to the very back of her mind.

When she left her grandfather's room, some twenty minutes later, she was surprised to find Andreas hovering near the head of the stairs.

'I brought your luggage up myself,' he said without preamble. 'If it had been left to either Sophia or Tomas, you would perhaps have been embarrassed.'

'Why?' Olivia suddenly realised that she did not know where to go. Which room had been prepared for her? Her cheeks flushed as she finally got the drift of the conversation.

'They fondly imagined that you would be back in our room, but realising that you have no more wish for that than I have, I've put your suitcase in the room you had before we were married.'

'I'm sorry to be so much trouble.' She couldn't look him in the eye. Once again she was reduced to being merely a child. She hardly felt old enough to be married at this moment, let alone have borne his son. A few minutes with her grandfather and now a veiled reprimand from Andreas and she was a blushing stammering schoolgirl again.

'I didn't realise they wouldn't have prepared a room. If there's anything to do, I can easily do it myself.'

'The room you used to occupy is always in a state of readiness, though woe betide anyone who would think of using it! Sophia and Alex would probably kill them. The room is a shrine, Olivia, didn't you know? They had nothing left but a room.'

He regarded her stonily for a second, seeing the tears start as she turned away and walked to the door of the room that had been hers alone for so long.

'Thank you.' She went inside anxious to get away from him, but he followed.

It was still the same, she had always loved the room, its pale pinks and creams a soft feminine background for either a teenager or a grown woman. After their marriage she had been reluctant to fully give up the room and for some time she had still kept some of her clothes in the long white wardrobe that was built into the wall facing the bed.

She still remembered her angry outburst on the day that Andreas had finally fetched all her clothes into the room that had become theirs, lying back on the bed as she ranted at him and telling her with a grin that her childhood was over and that as she now belonged to him, he would have all of her. He had accused her of wanting to remain a child for ever so that she could have the best of both worlds.

'I—I didn't realise that it was kept just the same,' she shot a quick glance at him and he stared grimly back.

'As I told you, it is a shrine. You clung to it yourself. What do you expect?' He looked with annoyance at her flushed face. 'Oh, don't worry, Olivia. I do not come to worship at the shrine.'

'I've got my case, so now you can go, thank you.' She walked further into the room, but he followed, ignoring her curt dismissal.

'How did you find your grandfather?'

'You're going in to see him yourself, aren't you?' she countered quickly, her face averted.

'Of course, but I asked how you found him.'

'Just the same, except for his obvious illness. I told him that Peter would be coming and he agrees,' she added quickly, turning to face him at last.

'Naturally!' Andreas sneered. 'He enjoys controversy, it brings added excitement to his life.'

'There'll be no controversy,' Olivia asserted firmly. 'At least I shall behave in a civilised manner, and no amount of dispute will alter the fact that in three months' time I shall be married to Peter.'

She was throwing down the gauntlet, she knew, but his cold face, his hard, dark eyes were altogether too much to bear at the moment.

'I have experience of your civilised behaviour,' Andreas ground out. 'Expect nothing from me, Olivia. You came here of your own free will and if you imagine that I shall be all sweetness and light to your lover, then you underestimate me.'

'Why are you pretending?' she cried out wildly, unable to keep up the barriers any longer. 'I wasn't the one to go to someone else. What do you think any wife would do when she found her husband with another woman?'

'That would depend on the maturity of the wife, I think,' he snarled derisively. 'My wife was a child who ran away, without faith, without even listening to reason.'

'Reason!' In her anger she stormed closer to his still figure. 'Perhaps if I hadn't already known why you married me I would have been prepared to listen, after you got your story sorted out, but don't forget I already knew that Grandfather forced you into marrying me, I heard it all!'

'You did?' His face was suddenly still and watchful. 'And you kept all this to yourself until now? What exactly did you hear?'

'I heard the quarrel, the quarrel you had with him the

week before he engineered that engagement. I couldn't hear properly, but I got the gist of it.' She paused for breath. 'I suppose now you'll add being a sneak to my other faults?'

Andreas smiled slowly, a sort of subdued elation on his face that she couldn't fathom.

'No, Olivia, I'm not going to call you a sneak. You were always wilful, wild, but I cannot envisage you with your ear to a keyhole. You were probably no closer than the top of the stairs, undoubtedly with your mouth open and your hands over your ears. You never liked quarrels, did you, and we were certainly laying into each other, as I remember.' He took a step closer and she felt the need to back away, to his obvious amusement.

'Tell me, little wife, why did you agree to marry someone who clearly married you against his will and better judgment? You were only eighteen and I was twenty-nine, almost thirty. Surely you realised what a handful you were taking on? I was not some mere manageable boy with my head in the clouds.'

She walked away, going to the window to hide her flushed face, her distress.

'I loved you,' she said quietly. 'I—I thought that one day you might love me as much. I hadn't reckoned with Leandi.'

'I could of course have refused to marry you,' he said softly. 'I have always been more than a match for your grandfather, and you know that well.'

'I don't know what that's supposed to mean,' she spun round angrily. 'I'm in no doubt as to why you agreed. The reality dawned on me painfully. You wanted what Grandfather wanted, the real heir to the Skouradis millions united with the heir apparent, any offspring in undoubted possession for ever!'

As soon as the angry words were out, she regretted them, praying that the blanching of her hot face as she

realised what her hasty words might bring to his mind,
would be mistaken for the white rage that he was so
used to in his own character.

For seconds he looked at her through narrowed eyes,
weighing her words. An image of Nicky flashed into
her mind, a minature image of his father, and Andreas
misinterpreted the swift spasm of pain that crossed her
face.

'Yes, Alex wanted it,' he said sombrely, 'and as I
doubted my ability to keep my hands off you any
longer, it seemed to be an ideal solution. As they say, it
seemed like a good idea at the time.' She stiffened as his
voice dropped to a deep murmur. 'I always wanted you,
Olivia—I still do.'

'What?' She was stiff with rage, her face white. 'If
you imagine for one moment that I would permit . . .'

'Permit?' He was upon her in two strides, grasping
her shoulders and jerking her to his hard chest. 'Permit?
You are my wife! Permission does not enter into it!'

Her breasts crushed against the iron wall of his chest,
Olivia still found the courage to reply, though his
nearness unnerved her.

'You Greek savage! What do you propose to do—
rape your ex-wife?'

Murder flashed in his eyes for one brief second and
she knew real fear. It was the first time that Andreas
had ever frightened her. True, she feared that he would
discover her secret—that he had a son—so like him that
since meeting him again she had felt the need to stare at
him until Andreas, Nicky and the old Andreas she had
loved to distraction were becoming mixed up in her
troubled mind, but she had never feared for herself until
now.

'You think it would be necessary?' The words were a
deep, dangerous growl.

Olivia stared into the glowing darkness of his eyes,
unable to move or utter a sound in her own defence as

the cruel grasp on her arms slackened to a light hold
and his dark head bent slowly to hers.

In spite of her mind's outrage, her body responded as
of old, tiny forgotten flames racing along her nerve
endings, tingling down her spine behind the subtle
caress of his stroking hands, like the white foam in the
wake of a boat.

Softly his lips teased hers, parting her lips, tasting the
long-remembered sweetness. His open palm ran down
the length of her spine and instantly desire stirred,
making her struggle to free herself.

'Panic, Olivia?' The white flash of his smile was close.
'A final bid for freedom?'

'I am free!' She struggled wildly, realising how
dangerous was his hold on her.

'Free until I call you.' With a sardonic smile, he
dropped his hands and she leapt out of his reach,
turning to face him, angrily at bay. He was playing with
her emotions, knew exactly what he was doing. It was
just another of his change of tactics. It meant nothing to
him. He had tried threats and scorn, recrimination, and
now he was trying this. Her hatred bubbled over the
top.

'Soon, Peter will be here. You've no power over me.'
She managed a little smile of triumph at the instant
savagery of his face, but her moment was shortlived.

'You are on my island.' His words were deceptively
soft.

'Grandfather's island!' she corrected waspishly, but
he shook his head slowly, his dark eyes gleaming with
victory.

'No, Olivia. You have been away too long. You've
lost the thread of things. Everything has been signed
over to me. The business and its troubles, the house, the
island—you are wrong to be so sure of yourself. My
island, Olivia, and my wife.' He smiled again as she
stared at him in fury.

'The smile on the face of a tiger!' she blurted out as he strode to the door.

'Very astute!' He turned to look at her, threat in his eyes, 'It pleased you to throw your rings at my feet, Olivia, and I have neither forgotten nor forgiven. I, on the other hand, retain my possessions, and I was possessive about you long before you were old enough to realise it. Perhaps you don't approve of my reasons for marrying you—nevertheless, I did marry you, so do not expect me to greet your lover with the false bonhomie of your English middle classes. When he steps on to my island I shall treat him in any way that I think fit and that is exactly how I shall treat you.'

'Grandfather gave his permission,' she reminded him.

'And I heartily agree with his decision.' He stood in the doorway, his eyes cold, his smile going no further than his thinned lips. 'Let him come. I am altogether too busy nowadays. I need some sort of diversion, and I'm sure that any fiancé of yours will make a wonderful distraction.'

He slammed the door and Olivia sank into the nearest armchair. She realised that her legs were shaking uncontrollably and that the wild beating of her heart was not entirely due to fright.

Was she such a fool that Andreas could capture her love again? She knew everything about him, his ruthless ways, his treachery, but her heart remembered his tenderness, the magic of his lovemaking, a magic she had been prepared to accept gladly only a few minutes ago if her head had not come to her rescue.

She covered her face with her hands. Her pilgrimage of mercy had turned out to be a very dangerous one indeed. Her logic told her that Andreas would not keep her here against her will, but her instincts told her that he would. Even if he let her go, his threat to follow her sounded real enough and she would lose Nicky.

She knew how Andreas would act. He would take

first and argue later from a position of strength. She had read how children of broken marriages had been snatched from their homes and taken to the country of one of the parents. Years sometimes passed before the law secured their release, and with someone as rich and powerful as Andreas, that time would never come.

She had lost Andreas, she would lose Nicky too, and that would be everything. She paced the room desperately. If only Peter were here now, he would know what to do. His common sense would lift her spirits. He would see some loophole, some simple thing that she was missing.

She stood up suddenly, her old determination restored. Just thinking about Peter helped. She was not alone. Andreas would find that he had a tiger by the tail too, because she wasn't a fool any longer and she wasn't going to let him win, to let him keep her here merely as a sop to his wounded ego.

If he wanted a wife, he could go ahead and marry Leandi, he was free now. He could have a son whenever he wished. Olivia banished that line of thought from her head swiftly. The pain that shook her at the thought of someone else having his children was too real to be dismissed, and she tried to wipe it from her mind when she realised that she was fast becoming her own executioner. It would be better not to think at all than to let her mind run in such dangerous and forlorn tracks.

CHAPTER FOUR

IT seemed that Andreas was not about to put into practice his stated intention to make life unpleasant for her, because for the rest of the day she saw nothing of him. Tomas too was nowhere to be seen, and Olivia concluded thankfully that some business on the island was keeping them both busy.

Dinner posed a problem. She knew that Andreas disliked eating alone, but she had no intention of sitting in isolated splendour at the other end of the long dining table while Andreas shot poisonous arrows of sarcasm in her direction.

Tomas lived in the house when he was on the island, but he had always refused to eat with the family, preferring to take his meals with Sophia, who while accepting her title of aunt, nevertheless refused even after all these years to count herself sufficiently part of the family to eat with the Skouradis males.

Olivia's excuse was her grandfather, and she informed Sophia that her dinner was to be served in her grandfather's room when he dined. What Sophia thought about it she did not know, because apart from a slightly exasperated gasp, the old lady said nothing, and Olivia knew that it was more than the other servants dared do to question her decision, Sophia would never permit that. She ran the household with a strict discipline that would not have been out of place in a convent.

Olivia found her grandfather somewhat subdued and spent most of the time entertaining him with her exploits since she had left the island. She avoided all mention of her life until she had moved to London. It would not do to have him question her time in Scotland, and to her relief, he made no reference to it.

The subject of Aunt Beth brought back the old familiar grin. He had not forgotten the pleasure he had gained from battling with that particular lady when she had stayed in Greece before the wedding.

'So, she now keeps house for you while you go out to earn your living?'

Olivia nodded, careful of her words, feeling on tricky ground here, but she need not have worried, only her own guilt made the subject dangerous.

'What did she think of your separation and divorce?' he asked unexpectedly, casting a quick look at her from beneath his shaggy eyebrows.

'She sides with Andreas.' Olivia's sigh of resignation was not lost on him, and his little grunt of satisfaction was evidence enough as to where his own loyalties lay.

'She is very much Greek in her outlook,' he said frimly, 'though not at all malleable. A strong woman, your aunt. A weakling would be well advised to have her on his side.'

His deep chuckle lightened Olivia's sombre mood a little. 'She admires you too,' she told him slyly. 'She has an overwhelming desire to box your ears.'

His shout of laughter startled her. She had expected that her sly dig would have annoyed him. It seemed that she did not know her grandfather as well as she had thought.

'A man could pass many enjoyable hours arguing with a woman like that,' he chortled, and seeing her astonished face, he patted her hand. 'You are too young, child, even now,' he said softly, 'but things will work out—they'll work out.'

'I agree,' Olivia was not about to be treated as a child any more. 'Peter and I will be married in three months and then my life will be settled at last.'

'I would not repeat thật to Andreas were I you, Olivia,' he advised darkly. 'He will not take it calmly.'

'I know, he doesn't relinquish his possessions readily,' Olivia snapped, gathering the plates together. 'He said that quite recently. But what he does not realise, Grandfather, is that I am not a possession, and I'm free as the air.'

Free as the air. Her temper carried her through the next few hours as she prepared for bed, but Nicky's face swam in her mind. She would never be free while that little face mirrored the image of his father, and it always would. Andreas was a life sentence.

Heavy-eyed and uneasy, Olivia came down the next day to find Andreas taking breakfast on the sunny patio outside the breakfast-room. His keen-eyed glance took in her tired face and worried expression before her rose and held a seat for her.

'Tea,' he ordered briskly as a servant appeared with speed. 'Madame Skouradis prefers it, and bring some fresh coffee, for me.'

'I wish you wouldn't call me that,' Olivia snapped. She was in no mood for a battle with Andreas, but she refused to let him get away with this.

'Force of habit,' he assured her briefly. He appeared about to say more, but another quick glance at her pale face stilled his biting tongue.

'What do you intend to do today?' he asked presently, calmly meeting her astonished look with dark, unreadable eyes.

'I'll talk to Grandfather, and maybe walk around the gardens.' Why he should care what she did was a mystery to Olivia. He hadn't cared what she did for the last few years.

'You cannot stay in the room with the old man during the whole of your stay,' Andreas asserted quietly. 'You look pale and tired, Olivia. You should treat this as a holiday, get a bit of sun. Working in a dusty office is not the best way to keep your health.'

'I didn't come for a holiday,' Olivia answered sharply. 'I came to see Grandfather. Had I wanted a holiday, this is the last place I would have chosen.'

His dark face darkened even more, but he said nothing for a moment, seeming to make a Herculean attempt to keep his temper in check.

'Tomas and I will be busy on the island today, as we were yesterday afternoon. You could come too if you wished. You could see the village and perhaps meet some of your old friends.'

'Ah!' She understood now the olive branch that he tempted her with. 'Thank you, but no, thank you,' she said quickly. 'I understand your desire to parade me in front of the village, the wayward wife returned to the fold, but regretfully I must decline to play that particular game. You must deal with your own deflated ego, Andreas. I intend to stay here for the whole of my stay. After all, if the poor villagers were to imagine that we were reconciled, then whatever would they think when I go again? Your stock as a macho Greek male would be even lower.'

He looked at her as if she was some sort of poisonous reptile, his glance disgusted and weary.

'*Theos!*' He put his coffee cup down and stared at her coldly. 'To think that I ever imagined for one moment that you were a woman! You are merely an insolent child.' He stood, prepared to leave, but his scornful eyes did not move from her flushed face.

'Do you know me so little that you imagine I care a damn what the villagers or anyone else thinks of me? I don't need the burden of you around my neck to convince them that I am a man. Those who know me will think that I am well rid of you.'

Olivia could find no answer to his biting words. Her head fell beneath the lash of his tongue and the contempt in his eyes, only a deep-seated pride keeping her tears at bay.

'For your information, Olivia, we are taking the boat round to the other side of the island to the old ruined village. Your trip among your old friends would have been short, and I remember how you loved the old village when you were a—child.' His hesitancy over the last word shamed her more. 'I had thought that a picnic lunch and a trip on the sea would perhaps have put some colour into your face, though I can see that there is plenty of colour in it now,' he added nastily. 'Therefore I will bid you adieu and leave you to your sulks.'

'I told you that I came only to see Grandfather,' she said huskily, unable to leave well alone.

'I remember.' Andreas paused at the door to the breakfast-room. 'Caring for your health and welfare is a habit that I acquired early. I shall have to get rid of it now that you have grown into a thoroughly unpleasant and ill-mannered female. Take your holiday in any way you wish.'

'I'll take it when Peter arrives, thank you.' She wanted to hurt back. To push from her mind the love he had given her when she needed it all those years ago, to remember only Leandi and his treachery.

'Perhaps he deserves you,' he said quietly. 'I wait with barely contained eagerness to see this unfortunate lover.'

'He's not my lover!' Olivia was on her feet, almost screaming at him. 'You know me well enough to know that I . . .'

'I don't know you at all, Olivia. I thought, long ago, that I did, but anyone, even I, can make a mistake.'

With this, the last word as usual, he left the patio, closing the door quietly, completely in control of himself, while Olivia sank shaking to her seat, her appetite gone. Had bitterness and pain altered her so much? She was ashamed at her outburst, angry with him for his ability to hurt her, frightened at the depth of feeling that he could force from her.

She did not see him for the rest of the day, and time hung heavily. Her grandfather slept in the afternoon and she wandered disconsolately around the fresh greenery of the gardens, standing at last on the cliff and looking out to sea, her eyes seeing nothing but the past, the *Anatoli* racing into the blue bay, her own long-legged figure at the helm with Andreas beside her guiding her hands, his arms reaching for her as they moored alongside the old pier.

There were other pictures too. The night of her grandfather's birthday party, the great house on the cliffs filled with lights and music, with guests from the other islands, from Athens, Rome and even further afield. There was excitement in the air and Olivia had faced the evening with great happiness, waiting for Andreas to see her in the new white dress she wore, its long full skirt adding an enchanting allure to her slender height.

She had gone down to the crowded rooms to find him, her face glowing with happiness—and then she had seen him with Leandi. They were in the shadows of the verandah, locked together in a passionate kiss, and her youth was a penance, a burden she had to bear as she pressed herself to the wall, her green eyes wide with despair.

At that moment Andreas raised his head, his own eyes stilling with shock as he met her stricken gaze, and then she was running, racing down the steps at the other end of the verandah, stumbling through the gardens and down the cliff steps to the moonlit beach.

She ran wildly, trying to outrun her pain, the sound of the sea and her own laboured breathing blotting out any other noise her hair flying behind her, her white dress billowing in the breeze. She looked like a slender stricken white bird seeking its own destruction.

She was beyond the view of the house when Andreas caught her. It had taken him seconds to recover, to realise her thoughts, and he was swift-footed, sure as a gazelle.

He caught her hair, slowing her down, and then threw one arm round her, tumbling her on to the soft dry sand. She fought him silently, tears spilling down her cheeks as she struggled beneath his weight, but his strong powerful body trapped her below him until she wore herself out and lay gasping for breath.

'Had enough?' He lay between her parted legs, his hands gripping her wrists as he held her arms half bent above her creamy shoulders.

'Let me go! Leave me alone!' The words were torn from her throat in a grief-stricken sob, and his hands slid over her palms, his skin stroking against hers.

'Why? Why should I let you go, *eros mou*?' His lips brushed hers, but she turned her face from him and his kiss slid warmly across her cheek.

'Don't touch me! I saw you! Go back to Leandi, go back to her!'

She was distraught, and his hands came to softly cup her face, holding her tightly as he pressed her into the sand.

'A goodbye kiss from an old friend, Olivia. I was not kissing her, she was kissing me. What should I have done, slapped her face? Called to you for aid?'

'It was you. I—I saw you! You were kissing her like—like a lover.'

'Like this, do you mean, *karithia mou*?'

The dark head swooped to hers and she stiffened beneath him, closing her teeth, making her mouth one hard straight line to defeat him, but his fingers caressed her cheeks, the scent of him, the very essence of him filled her nostrils, and when the tip of his tongue traced her stubborn lips, she surrendered with a small pain-filled cry as her arms wound around his neck, her lips parted to meet his searching kiss.

With a deep groan of obeisance, Andreas gathered her close, his arms warm and possessive, his lips moving over hers with growing passion, draining away her last resistance, driving the past and the future from her mind. There was only the sound of the sea, the moonlight on her skin, and Andreas.

'I didn't mean this to happen,' he groaned against her lips, 'not yet. Tonight is Grandfather's birthday, but it was to be your night, your dance, when all who did not already know it would be left in no doubt that you are mine.'

'Leandi . . .' she began, but he covered her lips with gentle fingers.

'Hush! I've told you the truth—a goodbye kiss. There is nothing between us. How can there be when I am mad for you?'

'I love you, Andreas.' Her little whisper earned her the reward of his lips. 'I do!'

For a second his fingers tightened round her slim throat and he looked at her with savage possession.

'Keep remembering that, Olivia,' he ground out, 'because I'll never let anyone else have you, I'll kill you first.'

He kissed her with a wild, Greek passion, his lips teaching her to respond, his hands caressing the length of her heated body, until for the first time she felt the shocking excitement of his own arousal and moved against him in innocent abandon, prepared to surrender everything in the dazzling light of love.

'Olivia!' he moved away from her and jack-knifed to his feet, looking down at the wild abandon of her body, the glorious disorder of her hair, the feverish green eyes.

'Come, sweet.' He reached for her, pulling her to her feet and straightening her dress.

'What did I do wrong?' She was shivering, and he pulled her into the warmth of his arms.

'You did nothing wrong. I drove you too far. I want

you, darling, but I'm going to wait, and therefore, so are you.' His breathing was less than steady and he turned to the house, his arm around her. 'Come, I'll take you back. They'll be expecting us.'

'Why should they be?' She clung to him, inviting and supple, her eyes filled with moonlight, and he looked away abruptly.

'You'll see.' He walked doggedly on and she went unwillingly, her hand in his, feeling that she had somehow injured him and at a loss to know what to do. She wanted to make things right before they reached the house.

'Stay here a little longer, Andreas,' she begged softly, and he stopped abruptly, his face taut as he looked down at her.

'Why?' His dark eyes were burning into hers and she looked away, her face flushed.

'To talk.'

'Talking is not what I want to do with you,' he rasped. 'The sooner we get home, the better. If we stay much longer then I can promise you, you'll be out all night.'

'I—I'm sorry,' she whispered, feeling that this was somehow all her fault and that Leandi would have handled it in a very different way.

'For what?' He suddenly pulled her hard against him, his breathing quickening instantly. 'For being utterly desirable? For being warm and willing in my arms? What are you going to do to prove that you're sorry?' He fondled the silken cloud of her hair, his lips planting butterfly kisses on her cheeks and mouth. 'Do you think you'll be able to stop enchanting me even if you try very hard, my little sweet?'

'I want you to love me like I love you.' She looked up into his eyes and with a low groan he put her away from him, taking her hand again and urging her on.

'You're mine, Olivia!' he said with the certainty of possession, and she had to be content with that.

She slipped in quietly by the side door and went to her room to repair the damage of her wild run, of the sand and of the scorching kisses that had left her lips full and swollen, going down at last to find Andreas waiting for her, his eyes going anxiously to her face, a look of tender concern on his own face that changed into a brilliant smile as she met his eyes.

They entered the *sala* at the end of her grandfather's birthday speech and he held out his hands to both of them, exchanging a long look with Andreas before announcing to everyone,

'Tonight, my friends, my happiness is complete, because this very evening, Andreas is to become engaged to my dear Olivia.'

She was pale with shock. It was true that she wanted this, that a deep happiness filled every part of her, but Andreas had never asked her to marry him. Her life had been arranged, and she knew, as she looked up into the fiercely possessive face of Andreas and then at the proud face of her grandfather, that this had always been her fate.

She had heard only part of the quarrel between them, but she had never expected this. Andreas had said that he was mad for her and she had realised that he wanted her badly. If he loved her enough to marry her then she wanted nothing else for the rest of her life.

Under the towering power of her grandfather, Andreas slipped the huge emerald ring on to her trembling finger, looking down at it for a moment and then planting a kiss on it.

'Mine!' he whispered softly, looking deeply into her eyes. 'Mine for ever, Olivia.'

They turned smiling to the guests, and it was then that Olivia saw the shock and near-panic in the eyes of Leandi and fear clutched at her heart. The Greek girl's eyes were filled with hatred, and it was a tangible force that swept across the room to Olivia. It was a threat and a promise, making her shiver, until she was drawn into the security of strong arms and looked up to find Andreas following her gaze, his face hard and equally threatening as he watched Leandi.

Then there were three months of bliss after she was married to Andreas. Days when he treated her with the indulgence he had shown her since childhood, nights when he taught her about love, warm moonlit nights when his insatiable desire left her weak and trembling until the stamp of his possession was marked on her soul.

Nothing, it seemed, could intrude on their happiness. Nothing could separate her from the husband whose dark eyes followed her every movement, smiling with indulgence or drowsy with desire.

They were staying for a few days in Athens when the world fell about her ears. A phone call she received at the apartment had her driving round to the office, eager to meet him at his command. She never knew who had telephoned—one of his staff, she had supposed. She had burst happily into the sumptuous office that Andreas reserved for himself, only to stop in horror, the smile frozen on her face at the sight of Leandi Kastakis clasped tightly in his arms, her head on his shoulder.

She had asked herself many times since then if her reactions had been normal, if she should have screamed at him, thrown things, but he had never said, 'I love you,'—not once. His eyes had shown naked desire, heated passion and the pride of possession, and Olivia had understood, after that hateful day when her life disintegrated, exactly where Andreas went to say, 'I love you.'

She was married to Andreas because her grandfather had ordered it so that she could bear the son who would one day rule this empire, but Andreas had chosen Leandi, chosen with his heart.

So the beautiful rings were thrown at his feet, the speed of her reactions amazing her, although it had seemed to be a nightmare in slow motion at the time. She had run and never stopped running, ignoring the harsh voice that called her name. She had not listened to his pleas when he had finally found her in the apartment, packing the few clothes she had brought with her. She had never gone back to Illyaros, in fact she had never spoken to him again until she had come home to Greece to see her grandfather.

When Nicky was born, she had wept, wanting Andreas to be there, but refusing to allow him to be sent for, determined to keep her son to herself, to rob him of this success. Her tears were shed privately as she held the beautiful child that Andreas had given her when he was unable to give her his love.

Well, she had Nicky. She turned away from her tormented contemplation of the still, green sea. He would never get Nicky. There would never be a time when Leandi Kastakis would have the right to take Nicky in her arms—and it was only a matter of time before Andreas married Leandi now, in spite of his empty threats.

Andreas did not return for dinner. Tomas came in and spoke to her for a few minutes, so Olivia knew that whatever they had been doing was now finished and she could guess where Andreas had gone. The *Anatoli* would be out, but she had more pride than to go and look.

She was poor company for her grandfather at dinner and excused herself early, taking the opportunity to slip down to the study and phone Aunt Beth while Andreas was away. She needed the reassurance of the sound of Nicky's voice. She needed to reaffirm to herself that she was doing the right thing, that her life was going exactly as she had planned it and that she did not need

Andreas. Nicky was rather tearful when she eventually
rang off and her feelings were rather guilty as she went
to bed. She had unsettled him merely out of selfishness.

Early next day, Tomas told her he had been ordered to
fetch her visitor from Athens. Olivia felt a quick flood
of relief. She had been gradually forgetting Peter in the
deep mixture of feeling that Andreas had managed to
arouse in her and she realised that a few more weeks
here and her life in London would have begun to seem
like a dream had it not been for Nicky. Too much of
her past was here, too much love and passion, it was the
most dangerous place. She had told her grandfather the
time of Peter's arrival and she felt that she had scored
some small victory at this.

'Did Grandfather tell you to go to the airport,
Tomas?' she enquired confidently.

'No. Kyrios Andreas ordered it yesterday.'

Her victory had been shortlived.

'I'll go with you then, Tomas, if you'll just wait for
me to change.' She was hurrying to the stairs when he
stopped her.

'I am sorry, Despinis Olivia, but I cannot take you
off the island. I am to fetch your guest, but you are not
to accompany me.'

'Andreas,' she remarked bitterly, glancing at Tomas'
red face.

'Yes. I am sorry, Despinis Olivia, but I cannot
disobey even for you.'

She nodded and waved him off, dragging a smile
for him from some store of fortitude she had not
realised she possessed. It was not his fault. She would
never ask him to disobey Andreas, but it confirmed her
belief. She was a prisoner until Andreas decided that
she could be free. She wondered what Peter's reaction
would be to this state of affairs and whether Andreas
would try to prevent her leaving when Peter left. The

law would not allow it, and Peter knew the law. This thought had to comfort her until she could see Peter, and she waited with impatience for his arrival throughout the rest of the morning and for long after lunch.

As the *Anatoli* came back across the rippling waters of the bay, Olivia sped down to the landing stage. Hope, comfort and safety was coming in on the boat and she could not calmly wait in the house.

Her greeting as Peter stepped from the boat was warmer than usual, fired as it was with desperation, not only the desperation of fear from herself, but the quiet desperation that had been growing every time she had seen Andreas.

She cared not that Tomas frowned his disapproval as she flung herself into Peter's ready arms, she cared not either if Andreas was watching from the house. She had not seen him today, but she knew his ability to anticipate anything and she was more than certain that he would have seen the arrival of the boat and her excited greeting of her fiancé. She was certain too that his black brows would be thunderous that her greeting had been conducted in front of Tomas. She didn't care, though; for the moment there was a modicum of safety, a promise of happiness.

'I expected to see you when I landed in Athens,' Peter said as they walked up the steps to the top of the cliff. Carrying one suitcase, his other arm around her, he looked down at her in surprise.

'I couldn't. I'll tell you about it later.'

'All right, my dear, it doesn't really matter, we're together now.' He hugged her to him and she felt grateful for his affection, pushing behind her the little devil that asked her in astonishment what she was doing with a feeling of gratitude when a touch from Andreas had once set her on fire, and still did now.

Her face paled as the object of her unwilling

thoughts paused on his way across the wide hall at their entrance.

'This is Peter Challoner.' Olivia hesitated and decided not to add 'my fiancé'. Things were bad enough as they were and she had no way of knowing how Andreas would greet Peter. She only knew what he had threatened.

'It's very nice of you to have me here.'

Olivia's skin flushed with anxiety. The words were urbane, the expected courtesy of any visitor to another man's house, but she heard the annoyance behind Peter's voice, he was having difficulty in speaking to Andreas at all.

Andreas looked at him for a long moment. She thought for a second that he was not going to answer at all. The dark eyes were cold and speculative, the handsome face enigmatic, only the slight tightening of his lips showed that he had heard the introduction and the suave greeting.

'You are the guest of my wife.' His voice was icy. 'It is unusual, but perhaps Greek hospitality can be stretched that far.'

'Ah, I see, the island belongs to Olivia's grandfather.' Peter's voice held controlled amusement. Clearly he had decided that Andreas held a no more exalted position here than did Olivia herself. Under these circumstances, dealing with Skouradis would be considerably easier.

'It does not!' Andreas said nothing further, but continued across to his study, pausing at the door, his superb body vibrant with aggression, his dark head turned once again to his unwelcome guest.

'Perhaps I had better warn you that during your stay, which I am given to understand will be for a little over a week, you will not be permitted to leave the island.'

'Why?' There was aggression too in Peter's normally well modulated voice.

'Because I have given those instructions to both my

staff and the villagers who own boats. I do not of course presume to deny you your personal liberty. If at any time you wish to leave, I will arrange for you to return to Athens—alone. Alternatively, you could always attempt the swim, the sea is reasonably calm at this time of the year.' His black brows lifted in amused appraisal at Peter's less than athletic build. 'I warn you, though, that I have not even tried that myself, but the English, I understand, often swim the Channel and it is very little farther to the mainland.'

Tiring of his amusement, he turned to Olivia.

'Dinner will be served at seven in the dining-room, see to it that you are there.' He closed the door on them, and Olivia turned to find Peter red-faced and almost open-mouthed.

'The arrogant swine!' He seemed about to explode, or worse still, follow Andreas into his study. 'What's all this about leaving the island—alone?'

'I'll tell you in a minute.' Olivia hurried him up the stairs. He had been allocated a room far from her own, for while her old room was almost immediately opposite the beautifully appointed room she had once shared with Andreas, Peter had been put at the far end of the long corridor. Whether Andreas had ordered this, or whether Aunt Sophia, in her outrage at a gentleman guest of the wife of her beloved Andreas being in the house, had made the decision herself, Olivia did not know.

Oddly enough, the arrangement suited Olivia, though she did not care to delve into the reasons why this should be so.

Following Peter into his room, she leaned against the door and waited for the interrogation that she knew would come.

'Well? What's all this about leaving alone—with his permission, of course?' He was annoyed, more aggressive than she had ever seen him.

'He refuses to let me go.'

Peter's eyes opened wide. 'Don't be ridiculous, Olivia! He may have said that, the man is obviously a bully, but the law is, after all, the law. You can leave whenever you wish, and you well know it.'

He seemed to be blaming her and for one moment she resented him until she realised that he was probably right. Once again she was under the shadow of Andreas, insecure and anxious. She had always been comfortable with him, but from the moment she had fallen in love with him, she had changed, she realised that although it had not seemed so obvious at the time. She had been the mouse to his cat, the petted and indulged possession that Andreas treated with almost feudal ownership. And she had resented it. Sometimes it had seemed that all the feelings were on one side only, her side. His desire for her had never been enough, his cossetting had never made up for the words of love that he had never spoken. It was hardly Peter's fault.

'Andreas is not a bully, and it's not as simple as you think.'

'That's twice I've heard you defend that swine,' he accused. 'Maybe you want to stay here and go through all that again?'

'You know I don't.' Olivia bit her lip. She was quarrelling with him and he had only just arrived. Damn Andreas! She had been defending him again. It seemed that she was willing to think anything she liked about his shortcomings, but she only had to hear another person attack him and she sprang to his defence like a she-cat. As if he needed her help to defend himself!

'He says if I leave, this time he'll follow me and see what I've been up to.'

'Good! Let him! He can come to the wedding.' Peter was red-faced with annoyance.

'Look, I know you're angry, Peter . . .' she began, but he cut her off brusquely.

'Angry? I'm bloody furious! I'm not accustomed to being treated in such a cavalier manner, as well you know, Olivia.'

He was a far cry from the calm, polite London solicitor, and Olivia sighed. Did Andreas do this to everyone? Bring out their deepest emotions? No, she reassured herself. He had business dealings all over the world, had been educated at Oxford, was truly cosmopolitan. The thought did not reassure her after all, because these waves only seemed to wash over her own life when Andreas touched it, waves that threatened to engulf her in their magnitude.

'I can't let him come to London, Peter, he'll find out about Nicky.' Her tired, unhappy face did nothing to quieten his temper and he spun round to glare at her.

'So? He can't touch the boy, he's not above the law.'

'You don't know him. He's powerful, ruthless. He gets everything he wants.'

'And he wants you!' He was up to her in a stride. 'Has he touched you? Has he been making love to you, Olivia? Is that what all this defeatist talk is about?' He was hurting her, and she pulled away.

'No! Are you mad? I hate him—he hates me too. He only wants to punish me.'

'Well, he can't do anything, talk's cheap.' He looked at her narrowly. 'I hope you know, Olivia, that you're neurotic about that boy.'

'He's not that boy! He's Nicky—my son!'

'Yes, and there are plenty of mothers who are alone. I see enough of that in my business. They pass through my office regularly, but none of them have this absurd passion that you have for that boy.' He stared hard at her. 'Of course, seeing Skouradis, I realise that Nicky is a miniature of his father. Is that it, Olivia? A wild desire to cling to what you have of Skouradis?'

'How dare you say that to me?' She whirled away,

making for the door, but he reached for her, clasping her in his arms.

'I'm sorry, darling, I'm jealous as hell.' It was uncharacteristic and it stopped her in her tracks. 'Let me hold you—I've missed you, darling.' His arms were hurting, but she submitted, hoping that his kisses would ease the tension, the hurt, but even as their lips met, she knew it wouldn't happen. She had seen Andreas again, been close to him and felt the rise of the old desire when he held her.

Tears began to sting her eyes and she pulled away as gently as she could. It would take a long time to get back into the calm frame of mind that Peter had got her to in three years. She would have to be back in England before the new hurt began to subside.

'Come down when you're ready, there'll be tea on the patio.' She left before he could stop her. There was enough misery, she was not about to inflict any on Peter. He deserved better than that.

CHAPTER FIVE

WHEN Olivia went on to the patio, Andreas was already there. Leaning against the delicate wrought iron rail that surrounded the tiled area with its pots of geranium and fuchsia, he stood looking out across the gardens, only turning his head momentarily at the sound of her steps on the echoing tiles.

Olivia was subjected to his intense gaze, his eyes sweeping over her slender figure before he turned away.

'You surprise me, Olivia,' he said tightly, his back to her. 'I imagined you would have better things to do with your time than take tea out here. Your reunion with your fiancé has been very brief. Tired, is he?'

She understood the innuendo but struggled to remain aloof.

'Not at all. Peter will be here shortly. Right now he's unpacking.'

'I can imagine.' Andreas turned, his eyes derisive. 'A strange choice for you, Olivia, or did you go for safety this time?'

'It's nothing to do with you!' She gave him an infuriated look which only served to amuse him further. 'The sort of person I choose to marry is none of your business.'

Instantly the dark eyes hooded, the thick curling black lashes flickering on to his cheeks as he lit a cigarette and watched the smoke from beneath lowered brows.

'Do you think I will permit you to re-marry? Do you think I am going to tamely hand over my wife to this pale-skinned weasel?'

The heated reply that sprang to her lips was stifled as

a maid came in bringing tea for Olivia, thick black coffee for Andreas and dishes of the sticky sweetmeats that Andreas seemed to be able to consume endlessly without gaining an ounce of weight.

The interruption gave her time to reconsider her reply.

'Our problems can be talked over in private.' She took a firm hold on her temper, wanting to spare Peter the embarrassment of all this. She was prepared to compromise. 'Whatever you want to say to me can be said when Peter isn't here.'

'Ah, you recognise him as an outsider?'

She handed him his coffee, trying to be as normal as possible. But his jibe had struck home more than he realised. She was beginning to think of Peter as an outsider. He no longer seemed to be the strong, comforting man she could lean on, a man to whom her future was dedicated. Almost without the realisation having sunk in, she was beginning to think of him as someone outside the family, a stranger who would be upset and angered by this endless, bitter battle between herself and Andreas.

'There's no reason to involve him.'

'Why?' His eyes narrowed cruelly. 'He is involved. He will suffer the consequences of moving into our lives.' He gave a twisted smile. 'If it is a strain on you, we can clear the air the moment he decides to put in an appearance.'

'Andreas! Please!' Olivia's hands curled in her lap as she became more agitated, and he suddenly muttered under his breath, tossing the half-smoked cigarette into the garden. Before she was aware of it he had placed his cup on the table and was beside her, looking down at her silky head.

'All right, Olivia.' Her head shot up at his quiet tone, her eyes widening at the look on his face. 'I'll spare you for now.' His hand swept with rough tenderness over her shining hair and then trailed teasingly across her pale cheeks.

'Don't!' Her whisper was weak as she stared up at him, her mouth dry. His touch was driving her wild, but he must never know it.

'Don't?' The soft dark eyes tormented her, his mouth seemed so close. 'Why not, my angel?'

'I'm not an angel!' Her attempt at sharpness came out all wrong. His nearness was driving the breath from her.

'Not an angel,' he conceded, 'but you're mine,' he added, well aware of her omission. His face was still now, his dark eyes wide open, glittering with an emotion that frightened her. 'You were always mine, Olivia. Even when you were a child there was no one else, and there never will be, will there?' His strong fingers grasped her chin. 'Will there?' he repeated harshly.

His fingertips moved softly to her neck, igniting little flames where they touched her sensitive skin, lingering in the low opening of her dress as if he hesitated to go further but seriously considered it.

'Andreas,' she whispered again, and his eyes narrowed at her obvious distress before he slid the offending hand behind her neck, tipping her face to his as he kissed her hard and fast on the lips.

She heard Peter's footsteps as Andreas lifted his head and her face flushed in anger.

'You're despicable!' She sprang to her feet and faced him like a creature at bay, bitterly ashamed that she had welcomed his lips, had made no attempt to struggle. 'You saw him coming, didn't you?'

He nodded, his white teeth bared in a tigerish grin.

'Why not? Let him see that you are my wife,' he cupped her face in warm hard hands, 'because Olivia, I'll never let you go.'

His eyes were on her waxen face, her troubled,

shadowed eyes, as he released her and moved back to the edge of the patio. He barely glanced up as Peter strode forward, he seemed suddenly to have descended into some sombre mood of his own.

'Keep your hands off Olivia!' The rage on Peter's face showed clearly that he had witnessed the scene as Andreas had intended. 'Don't touch her ever again!' He was struggling with an inner violence that Olivia would not have expected ever to witness.

'Ever?' Andreas turned slowly, resting back against the rail, his lips twisted in a sardonic smile. 'You surely do not expect me not to touch my own wife? I'm a little too hot-blooded for that.' His taunting words drove Peter on and he shook off Olivia's restraining hand.

'In three months' time this little nonsense will be over, Skouradis. Olivia will be married to me and there's not a damned thing that you or anyone else can do about it!'

Knowing him as she did, Olivia was not deceived by the calm of Andreas; he was slowly burning, a murderous rage behind his still, dark eyes.

'She is mine, has always been mine! I do not misplace my possessions!' The malevolence he directed at the fair-haired Englishman was frightening, but Olivia was incensed. She was tired of being batted about like a ball between two unfeeling men.

'I'm not a possession, yours or anyone's!' she yelled.

'Be quiet, Olivia!' Andreas raised his voice above hers, his intense dark eyes scorching her, but she would not be silenced, she was no child now.

'Don't raise your voice to me, you animal! Peter never shouts.'

Unexpectedly, he was amused. The anger left his face as the glittering eyes swept over her. 'I can imagine that very well. You've become a power in your own right, *karithia mou*. You prefer a whining deferential approach now, do you? I can see that you would probably get it from him, but never from me, wife.'

With a minor explosion of sound, Peter stepped forward, his fists clenched, but Olivia sprang between them.

'Don't, Peter, that's just what he's waiting for.'

'Then that's what he'll get!' His teeth clenched, the normally urbane face suffused with angry colour, he pulled free of her frantically grasping hands, but she grabbed his sleeve again.

'He'll kill you, Peter.'

The quiet certainty stopped him more effectively than her clinging hands. Andreas had not moved, his face was impassive, but there was a danger about him that anyone would ignore at their peril.

'You still know me well, Olivia.' Apart from a tense waiting in the superb lean body, he appeared not to have reacted, but the dark eyes were narrowed in anticipation as his goading continued. 'Caution is wise. Is he cautious in bed too?'

'Don't dare talk like that in front of Olivia!' Though shaking with rage, Peter held back. He saw now what Olivia had seen at once, the stark danger of those glittering eyes. 'If you're implying that she and I . . . that we . . . I have more respect for her!'

'Ah!' The tight smile was turned on Olivia and her face flamed. 'So, you told the truth. Very interesting. Perhaps your "friend" and I have more in common than I realised. I had respect for you also—once.'

'But not for long!' She bit out the words angrily and saw the cold flare of rage in his eyes. It seemed that they were alone on a tight, pain-filled island of their own making, battling to hurt each other in a fight to the death.

'No. As I remember, my respect for you lasted for those brief months of marriage, and then you reverted to childhood and ran. You fled without reason, without courage, without faith. My respect died then, Olivia. Expect from me now whatever I care to dish out.'

He turned to the door and her temper and hurt flared over, the injustice choking her.

'Go to hell!'

'Not without you, *karithia mou*,' he said softly, turning a sneering smile on her. 'Wherever I go, we go together.'

'Threats will do you no good, Skouradis. There's such a thing as the law,' Peter intervened belatedly, but Andreas smiled more widely, his black brows raised.

'The law? Here, I am the law. Tread softly, Englishman.' Peter opened his mouth, but Olivia forestalled him.

'Ignore him, Peter,' she advised with biting sarcasm, 'he's a legend in his own imagination.'

To her astonishment this remark brought the gleaming dark head round to her and she found herself at the receiving end of a flashing smile of sheer amusement.

'Impudent witch!' Andreas' eyes swept over her possessively. 'That sounds more like my woman. Oh, you're certainly mine, Olivia.'

He strode from the patio, the sheer force of his personality, his shattering arrogance keeping both Olivia and Peter silent for minutes after his steps had died away.

'He can't do anything, Olivia.' Peter strove to regain his shaken self-esteem. 'Don't worry, darling.'

'I'm not worried!' She shook off his tentative hold and walked to the rail of the patio. 'I could kill him! I really could! Of all the insufferable, big-headed, contemptible . . .'

'Darling, this is not like you, you've let him upset you.' He came across to her, but she was in no mood to be either placated or to back down.

'You can't understand, Peter,' she snapped, the only deep thought in her mind being Andreas and the need to get the better of him, preferably with physical violence. 'Andreas knows how to goad me. I'm half Greek myself, you know.'

There was an unknowing pride in her angry voice, a link with Andreas, and it dawned on the man who watched her that he was merely an onlooker in a very private battle. The thought was not welcome.

There was a wildness about Olivia, a noticeable sensual beauty that made her seem brilliantly alive as she stood fuming by the rail of the patio.

Only Andreas could do this to her. Only he could bring out the deepest emotions that ate at her. She was in torment—a mixture of ferocious anger and utter bewilderment.

Why was he so angry? Why had he looked so capable of killing Peter? She ran through a list of reasons in her head, but every answer that she came up with seemed inadequate in the face of such violence.

He had been on the edge of violence ever since they had met in Athens, and bitter and angry as she was herself, she could not really see why he should be so close to fury all the time. He knew nothing of Nicky, so what was her crime? She had left him, but he was not an uneducated peasant, he knew the reason why.

He discounted the divorce, despised her for running away, but he knew why, after all, he had been there at the time—it had been his arms that held Leandi. He had said that he hated her and yet he intended to keep her here. Why? She was as furious with him about the whole mysterious business as she was with his extreme arrogance.

Next morning, after a restless night, Olivia was dressing as Sophia burst into the room. Her nerves were so on edge that for a moment she thought it was Andreas.

Dinner the previous night had been a nightmare. With Peter there she had been unable to defy Andreas and retreat to her grandfather's room for her meal.

They had sat in almost total silence. The place settings spaced around the long table had made it impossible to speak quietly to Peter, and Andreas, sitting at the head of the table, had not spoken once. His eyes had been on her all the time until her nerves were screaming and her face was as pink as a wild rose.

'There's a phone call for you, Olivia.' Sophia, quite out of breath, stopped in the doorway. 'It's in the study,' she apologised as Olivia's hand went out to the extension by her bed. 'I forgot to put it through. Your Aunt Beth sounded so upset that I ran straight up.'

'It doesn't matter.' Olivia was already racing out of the room. They had agreed that once she was on the island, Olivia would get in touch as often as possible. Knowing that any calls to the house would increase the risk of Andreas finding out about Nicky, Aunt Beth would never phone except in an emergency.

'Aunt Beth? What is it?' A quick glance around the hall had shown that Andreas was not about and she felt reasonably safe.

'Oh, Olivia, thank goodness! I've had such a night with Nicky.' Aunt Beth sounded exhausted, and anxiety made Olivia's voice rise louder and higher.

'What is it? What's wrong with him?'

'Nothing, Olivia. Don't go upsetting yourself! He's perfectly all right, but he can't settle. All night he's been crying and fretting, I guarantee he hasn't slept more than an hour. He wants to see you, or at the very least, to hear your voice.'

'Oh, Aunt Beth!' Tears were already starting in Olivia's eyes. 'Oh, I honestly wish I'd never come. It's a long time for a little boy. I'll try to get back tomorrow. Is he there now?'

'Yes, hanging on to my skirts. If he wasn't so exhausted you'd hear him yelling. He's got a fine temper, this one!'

Yes, become a Harlequin home subscriber and the celebration goes on forever.

To begin with we'll send you:

- **4 new Harlequin Presents novels – Free**
- **an elegant, purse-size manicure set – Free**
- **and an exciting mystery bonus – Free**

And that's not all! Special extras – Three more reasons to celebrate

4. Money-Saving Home Delivery That's right! When you become a Harlequin home subscriber the excitement, romance and far-away adventures of Harlequin Presents novels can be yours for previewing in the convenience of your own home **at less than retail prices.** Here's how it works. Every month we'll deliver eight new books right to your door. If you decide to keep them, they'll be yours for only $1.75! That's 20¢ less per book than what you pay in stores. And there is **no charge for shipping and handling.**

5. Free Monthly Newsletter – It's "Heart to Heart" – the indispensable insider's look at our most popular writers and their up-coming novels. Now you can have a behind-the-scenes look at the fascinating world of Harlequin! It's an added bonus you'll look forward to every month!

6. More Surprise Gifts – Because our home subscribers are our most valued readers, we'll be sending you additional free gifts from time to time – as a token of our appreciation.

*This beautiful manicure set will be a useful and elegant item to carry in your handbag. Its rich burgundy case is a perfect expression of your style and good taste. And it's yours **free** in this amazing Harlequin celebration!*

HARLEQUIN READER SERVICE
FREE OFFER CARD

4 FREE BOOKS

ELEGANT MANICURE SET – FREE

FREE MYSTERY BONUS

PLACE YOUR BALLOON STICKER HERE!

MONEY SAVING HOME DELIVERY

FREE FACT-FILLED NEWSLETTER

MORE SURPRISE GIFTS THROUGHOUT THE YEAR – FREE

☐ **YES!** Please send me my four Harlequin Presents novels **Free,** along with my manicure set and my **free mystery gift.** Then send me eight new Harlequin Presents novels every month and bill me just $1.75 per book (20¢ less than retail), with no extra charges for shipping and handling. If I am not completely satisfied, I may return a shipment and cancel at any time. **The free books, manicure set and mystery gift remain mine to keep.**

108 CIP CAKN

FIRST NAME   LAST NAME

(PLEASE PRINT)

ADDRESS   APT.

CITY   PROV./STATE

POSTAL CODE / ZIP

HARLEQUIN "NO RISK GUARANTEE"
* There is no obligation to buy – the free books and gifts remain yours to keep.
* You pay the lowest price possible – and receive books before they're available in stores.
* You may end your subscription anytime–just let us know.

PRINTED IN U.S.A.

Remember! To receive your four free books, manicure set and surprise mystery bonus return the postpaid card below. But don't delay!

DETACH & MAIL CARD TODAY

BUSINESS REPLY CARD

First Class   Permit No. 717   Buffalo, NY

Postage will be paid by addressee

Harlequin Reader Service
901 Fuhrmann Blvd.,
P.O. Box 1394
Buffalo, NY 14240-9963

NO POSTAGE
NECESSARY
IF MAILED
IN THE
UNITED STATES

'Let him speak to me.' It was hard to contain the tears. All she wanted was her arms around the cuddly little body, the scent of his warm hair in her face.

'Hullo, Nicky?' He started to cry at once and Olivia's tears spilled over. 'Don't cry, Nicky. Mummy's coming home at once, by tomorrow, I promise.' She didn't know how she was going to do it, but she was, even if she had to steal a boat. 'Don't cry, darling, I'll see you soon.'

His distress was so great that the only word he was capable of was, 'Mummy,' and Olivia could hardly control her own misery. For a second she pressed her hand to her mouth and stifled the sobs as she listened to the incoherent little voice so far away.

'Olivia!' The strong arm that came round her shoulders was frighteningly familiar and she raised a startled, tear-stained face to his, her fright miraculously drying her tears. She must have forgotten to shut the door. She had not heard him approach, and her mind frantically ran through the last few seconds of her conversation. How much had he heard?

'What's the matter? Why are you so upset? Is it your aunt?' His concern for her only served to make her more agitated and she shook her head, unable to speak, ramming the receiver against her ear, terrified that he would hear the little voice at the other end.

'Olivia! Let me help you. Tell me why you're so distressed.' When she failed to answer, he took the phone from her tight grasp, holding her away when she tried to stop him.

Olivia didn't need to be told what he heard. The sheltering arm dropped from her shoulders and the look he turned on her had the coldness of death. Without a word he handed the phone back to her and walked from the room.

'Nicky?' Her voice was breathless, but she had to ease the little mind. 'Mummy has to go now, darling, but I promise to see you tomorrow. Mummy's coming home.'

She went straight back to her room when she had put the phone down. She had to have some time to think, to lock her door and work out some kind of plan. In her mind she could not work out either the tenderness that Andreas had shown her when she was so clearly upset, or the reason he had walked off without a word.

She was left in no doubt about the latter as she hurried into her bedroom. As she turned, it was to see Andreas waiting, and she had no need to lock the door, he did it for her with the speed of a panther.

'My son!' He pushed her hard against the door, his face contorted in wild rage. 'My son, you cheating little bitch!'

'He's not!' she lied wildly. 'He's only two, he's nothing to do with you.'

'Two and what, Olivia?' He grasped her face cruelly, his weight pressing her into the door. 'Two years and what?' He released her face and grasped her shoulders, his fingers biting into her delicate bones. 'Don't expect me to swallow the idea that the child I just heard on the phone, crying for his mummy, is the son of that white-faced creature I met yesterday, the one who reacted with such virginal outrage when he imagined that I thought he had slept with you!'

Olivia stared at him like a rabbit trapped in the headlights of a car—indeed, she felt that at any moment he would destroy her. His grip tightened and he shook her until her head lolled about on her neck like a flower on a weak stem.

'Answer me, you underhand little bitch!'

'It was somebody else,' she improvised wildly and unwisely. 'I hated you when I found out about Leandi. I had an affair with somebody else.'

For a second she feared that she had gone too far, that Andreas would kill her then and there, but his eyes narrowed thoughtfully and although the punishing grip did not slacken, the moment of danger passed.

'Somebody else?' His face came close to hers, his eyes threatening. 'Pray hard, Olivia,' he growled. 'Pray hard that when I see your son he looks enough like me to convince me that he is mine and that all this is a frantic lie to get you off the hook. Because if he should be anything but my son, if you have let anyone else have you, the only way you'll leave this island is dead!'

He thrust her from him and strode from the room, his face white with rage, and Olivia lost precious seconds recovering from the fury of his onslaught.

'Aunt Beth!' She raced across to the phone. 'I've got to warn her.' But she was too late already. As she lifted the receiver she could hear Andreas on the phone in the study. He was ordering his plane to be made ready at Athens, and she had no doubts about his destination.

He finished his call and then spoke to her.

'Get off this line, Olivia! I have given orders that no outgoing calls of any nature are to be accepted during my absence, so as an instrument of communication this channel is useless to you until I return from England.'

She dropped the phone back into its cradle and raced downstairs to see him just coming from the study.

'Take me with you, Andreas!' She was not above begging when Nicky was at stake, and the cold dark eyes registered the fact with grim satisfaction.

'Take you with me?' His voice was a quiet, frightening sound. 'I've told you that you will remain here.' He walked forward and grasped her hair, jerking her towards him until she was crushed against the unyielding hardness of his chest. 'If the child is not mine, then I'll kill you for giving to another man that which is mine alone. And if he is my son, I'll not forget that you were prepared to marry that English jellyfish and share my child with him. Either way you lose, Olivia—either way I'll punish you.'

He released her so abruptly that she fell to the floor, and he strode away immediately, mounting the stairs two at a time, oblivious of her sobbing, concentrating only on getting to London with all possible speed.

She didn't try to approach him again. He had made his position quite clear and she dared not seek out Peter until Andreas had left the island. His rage was now such that she felt worried about Peter's safety should Andreas find her consulting him.

It was only when she knew he had left the house that she hurried to Peter's room, to find him coming out on his way to breakfast.

'He's found out! Peter, he's found out!'

'Calm yourself, Olivia.' He was back in his skin of solicitor and her heart sank. 'I imagine you're talking about Nicky, as you're so agitated.'

'Andreas has gone to get him.'

Olivia suddenly felt dully submissive. What was the use? There was no way to defeat Andreas. Here on his own ground he was invincible. Any plans she made would have to be made in secret. She knew with certainty what she had long suspected, that Peter did not relish the idea of being father to another man's son.

She had no doubt whatever that Andreas would find Nicky, and she could expect no help from her grandfather. He was also getting what he wanted at long last.

'What do you want me to do?' Peter's question startled her for a minute, but she had a grip on herself now. It was unfair to involve Peter in all this, he had no realisation of the passions that ran like wildfire through this house. To compare him with Andreas was unfair too. Anyone came out badly in comparison with Andreas. She had never in her life seen anyone capable of standing up to him. She supposed that Peter was an attraction for her because he was to all intents and purposes the very antithesis of Andreas—calm, quiet, a sort of refuge. She bit her lip as she realised the selfishness of her thoughts. He was a barrier that she stood behind, a barrier to hide her from all thoughts of Andreas.

'It's all right Peter, there's nothing that anyone can do. Andreas will get Nicky and nobody can stop him.'

'I wouldn't say that.' He sounded disgruntled that Andreas Skouradis should be considered to be above the law. However, there was a certain satisfaction in his voice.

'You're very wise, Olivia, to resign yourself to the inevitable. Much as I detest him, he is the boy's father. Surely you realise the advantages for Nicky to be heir to all this?'

'I know. Maybe it's for the best that I came here and Andreas found out about his son.' Olivia didn't feel like that at all, but there was nothing to do about the situation at the moment and there was no point whatever in being angry with Peter or involving him in her secret plans. After all, she hadn't gathered her wits about her sufficiently yet to make any. She only knew that there was no way that she would surrender Nicky to Andreas. Even without the certainty of Leandi in the background she could never leave Nicky here, he would be lost to her.

Just because she was not being subjected to the presence of the Greek girl it did not mean that she was no longer in the picture—her recent night in Athens had proved that conclusively. Andreas had always been discreet and she hardly thought that her grandfather would approve of seeing another woman on the island with Andreas. Her grandfather loved her, she was certain of that if of nothing else.

'Sensible girl!' Peter put his arm around her and gave her a brief hug, satisfaction in his voice. 'Once he gets the boy over here, he'll be only too glad to see the back of both of us.'

'You're wrong there, Peter.' She walked out into the blaze of sunlight on the patio. 'Andreas will never let me go, he wants me too.' If only to punish me for the rest of my life, she added to herself.

'You're being dramatic, darling. He seems to pack a fair amount of hatred into everything he says to you. I doubt if he'll be concerned once he has the boy.'

'Perhaps not.' It was a pointless discussion and she was glad of the diversion as he turned away at the sound of the helicopter rising above the hill beyond the house.

'What's that?' Peter was momentarily deflected from his purpose in reassuring her.

'It's Andreas. The helicopter is always kept here for emergencies. He'll meet his plane in Athens and be back here before nightfall.'

'Why on earth didn't you say about the chopper? We could have maybe bribed the pilot to take us to the mainland.'

'Bribed the pilot?' Olivia turned pitying eyes on him. 'The pilot is Andreas. I very much doubt if he could be bribed into anything, unless it was to take us out over the sea and jettison us.'

They both turned to look up as the silver and red machine rose smoothly into the sky and turned out to sea. The Skouradis colours, she would have known it anywhere even without the name blazoned proudly across the glittering silver of the sides.

She had flown many times with Andreas and knew his skill. Within twenty minutes he would be at the controls of his own jet and already the Skouradis minions in London would be tracking down Nicky. By the time Andreas arrived he would only have to walk in, charm Aunt Beth and walk out with his son in his arms. He was like the heartbeat of a well-oiled machine. He would have Nicky and be back on the island before night fell.

'Let's sunbathe by the pool.'

Clearly Peter had decided that they should behave calmly and expected her to show little reaction to the incidents of the morning. He was unable to hide the fact that the removal of Nicky from England gave him a satisfaction. It was a part of their lives neatly tied up and she wondered how he could be so unfeeling when he knew what keeping Nicky meant to her.

'No, I'm a bit restless, as you can imagine. You go ahead, I'll join you later.'

Of course he went, and in this too, her treacherous mind began to compare him with Andreas. Had the positions been reversed, Andreas would have been smashing mountains to help her.

She walked off dejectedly into the gardens, scarcely aware of her surroundings, starting nervously as a powerful figure detached itself from the trees and fell into step beside her.

'I expected that you would have gone with Andreas.'

'No, he left me to guard you,' Tomas said quietly.

'To spy on me, don't you mean?' She whirled on him, her eyes flashing with annoyance, but he shook his head sadly.

'To watch over you is not to spy on you, Despinis Olivia. There are many things that you do not know, but one thing you should never have forgotten is that I would not harm you in any way, even if Andreas ordered it. To spy on you would be unthinkable, dishonourable.

He looked completely saddened, and she felt a rush of affection for this kindly, ugly man who had been her constant companion and help since childhood.

'Oh, Tomas, I'm sorry.' She slid her arm into his and matched her steps to his stride. 'There are things that you don't know either, but you'll know soon enough.'

She tried to brighten up for both their sakes. It was no use moping. The game was being played and

Andreas held all the cards for the moment. 'Let's walk to the old village. That should keep us out of mischief for the moment, at least until lunchtime.'

'And long after,' he grinned. 'It's a fair walk. We'll both be in need of a rest this afternoon.'

'All the better,' she said quietly. It would be a long day.

They never made it to the old village. By the time they had reached the ruined fort that marked the edge of the old harbour, they were both tired and Olivia's conscience was getting the better of her. She had simply abandoned Peter, preferring the company of Tomas, and as they rested for a few minutes, sitting on the crumbling old walls and looking out across the blue glitter of the old harbour to the ruins of the village that stretched along the opposite shore, she realised just how deeply she had been drawn back into her old life, her old loves.

Lunch had already been served when they returned to the house and Olivia was not surprised to find Peter in a bad mood, his skin painfully pink from too much sun too quickly, and it was not long before he pleaded a headache and went to his room.

She tried to rest herself, but found it impossible, and her feeling of guilt grew when she realised that she had not been in to see her grandfather today. Her battles with Andreas seemed to be taking over all her waking hours, and she hurried along to her grandfather's room torn between pouring out her story to him and keeping quiet.

In the event she said nothing about Nicky. He might have heard the quarrel between herself and Andreas, but it was nothing new to hear Andreas raise his voice, his ready temper was something that they all lived with, just as his ready laughter had once been a constant factor also.

'You look tired, Olivia.' Her grandfather eyed her with concern. 'Are you sleeping properly?'

'Of course. Who wouldn't in this beautiful air?' She turned the conversation quickly. She didn't want him to probe into her tiredness. 'I've been walking with Tomas to the old fort. Everything's just as it used to be,' she added.

'Naturally.' He looked at her steadily from beneath his shaggy brows. 'Things settle down, become tranquil, life has a way of levelling things up.'

'My mother used to say that.' Olivia suddenly felt again the loss of her parents even after all these years. 'She used to say that when God closes a door, he opens a window.'

He smiled briefly and sadly. 'Yes, it seems so short a time since she sat at my feet on this stool. She was fiery too, just like you. It seems too only like yesterday that you too sat beside me out on the verandah, watching the sea, waiting for Andreas. There was a wonderful affection between you. A good basis, one would have thought, for a long and happy marriage.'

She chose to ignore his last remark and carried the footstool out on to the verandah, coming back with a bright smile to push his chair out into the sunshine.

'Let's do it again, then. Let's watch the sea and you can tell me some of your old stories.'

Her grandfather gave his great bark of a laugh, but readily complied.

'I don't tell many stories nowadays, Olivia.' His rough old hand stroked her hair as she settled beside him, leaning against his legs and narrowing her eyes against the brilliance of the sun on the shimmering water. 'I would like to help you, *pethi*, but it seems that both you and Andreas have grown beyond my reach.'

'Why, I don't need help, Grandfather. My life is running along nicely.' She almost told him about Nicky, but couldn't bring herself to do it. Time enough when Andreas came. At least the old man was in for a pleasant surprise, and she doubted if it would be too much for him, she was beginning to think that he was indestructible.

'You think that Andreas has changed?' It was a quietly spoken question, but her guard went up instantly.

'Not really. He's changed from what I used to think he was, and perhaps the worries of the business have hardened him a bit. Basically though, I suppose he's the same. I used to think he was different when I was younger, with my head in the clouds and my feet heading for the most enormous hole.'

She finished on a touch of bitterness that she was unable to conceal, and he sighed, shaking his head.

'You think that he is ruthless, perhaps cruel, yes? Maybe you should remember him as he was and ask yourself a few questions. He carries the flag now, like it or not. Everything he has done has been for you, and now he seems to have lost you. I'm not very surprised to hear his voice raised.'

'What are you talking about?' Olivia grasped his arm, but he only grinned sheepishly and patted her hand.

'I'm an old man, *pethi*. Old men often wander in their minds. Ignore me, I'm only thinking aloud.'

'You're an old rogue.' Olivia looked at him narrowly. A few more words and he would have blurted out something that she instinctively felt was of great importance to her. If only she had kept quiet—she had never learned to hold her tongue, and she could tell by the shuttered expression on his face that Alex Skouradis had firmly gripped his own runaway tongue. She would get nothing out of him now. It made her feel less guilty about letting him wait to be told about Nicky. If he knew anything that she should know, then it was his duty to tell her, but just like Andreas he made sweeping decisions and arrogantly stuck to them. They had both always treated her as a child and no amount of pleading would move them once they had come to a decision.

Everybody, it seemed, thought they knew what was best for her.

She left him soon after that and time hung heavily as the golden day drew into evening. After a long rest, Peter came downstairs refreshed and in a more even frame of mind, but she was a poor companion, her thoughts were constantly in London, fretting and conjecturing about the actions that Andreas would take, and she could not confide in Peter, he was happily settled to the idea that Nicky would remain here as heir to all the Skouradis millions and that Olivia would marry him and fit smoothly into his life without the unthinkable distraction of a small child to upset the smooth tenor of his existence.

It was seven o'clock before she heard the sound that she had waited for all day, the thrashing of the blades of the silver bird as it flew over the house and then the engine of the Land-Rover as Tomas went out to meet Andreas. Nicky would be there too, she never doubted that for a moment. Without him, Andreas would not be returning.

Even so, it seemed like an hour before she heard the slam of car doors and stopped pacing restlessly up and down the *sala*. She dared not go out to meet them, some inner dread kept her firmly rooted to the spot, and she was aware of Peter's disgruntled gaze upon her as she stood clenching and unclenching her anxious fingers, waiting for the door to open.

Then suddenly he was there. The door opened and Andreas stood looking at her, his dark face filled with a radiance that she had never seen before, his son curled in his arms, the little hands clinging to his neck.

They were so alike. Olivia's heart almost stopped as she saw the two of them together. The two people she loved most in the whole world—her heart admitted it, and she was afraid to look at Andreas in case he saw all too clearly what she felt for him.

Nicky stirred sleepily and the little face lifted to rest against the darker face of his father. He opened his eyes and for a second they both looked at her, both exactly alike. Andreas smiled slowly. For now all his anger was forgotten and the eyes that looked at her were the eyes of an Andreas she had lost long ago.

'Mummy!' Nicky saw her and the spell was broken.

She hesitated, unsure of her position, but Andreas came forward, placing the sleepy child in her arms, smiling as she buried her face in the cloud of dark hair, as the little arms clung tightly to her neck.

'Mummy, at last!' Andreas laughed, and as she looked up at him, he nodded quietly. 'He's beautiful, Olivia.'

'He's exactly like you—I mean . . .'

'I know what you mean.' His soft laughter tingled down her spine. 'He's beautiful and he's Greek.' He tipped her chin up and smiled into her startled eyes. 'Just like his father. Yes?'

He strode across to pour himself a drink.

'I need this. That young man is one handful, very wilful.' Olivia met his eyes over the top of Nicky's head, her eyebrows raised, a half smile on her face, and he looked back, grinning ruefully.

'Don't say it. I know.' There seemed to be just the three of them in the whole world for this moment. Peter was ignored, their bitterness forgotten as their eyes locked together. Only the contented crooning of the small boy, the exciting presence of the tall, dark man who had fathered him and the slender beauty of the tawny-haired girl who rocked him in her arms.

Andreas raised his glass, his eyes narrowed and glittering with an intensity she had never seen before.

'To you, Olivia,' he saluted softly, 'and to our beautiful son. Thank you.'

Peter stirred restlessly on his seat by the window and Andreas seemed to notice him for the first time.

'Ah, the fiancé!' He looked at him as if he had just discovered something very nasty in the room. 'A slightly brighter colour than when I last saw him, but the same person nonetheless.'

He looked quickly across as Olivia made a little sound of distress. She couldn't face an outburst from either of them just now, and Andreas seemed to read the appeal in her wide eyes, because he put his drink down and came across, lifting the drowsy child from her arms.

'We must present him to Alex. Come, little tiger. Meet your great-grandfather.'

'Mummy!' The wail of protest was stilled as Andreas settled him against his shoulder, his deep voice soothing.

'Mummy is here, nothing to worry about.' Andreas' voice was firm and certain, and the shrill little cries stopped. 'No more partings.' There was a finality to the words that silenced Olivia too, and when he took her hand to lead the way, she went willingly.

CHAPTER SIX

'HAVE you told Alex?'

Andreas seemed suddenly to realise that he was holding her hand and his hand fell away from hers as they climbed the stairs.

'No.' She felt guilty that she had not, but the whole afternoon, the waiting and the fear had been almost unbearable as it was.

'Why? You were never a coward, Olivia.' He glanced at her and she looked quickly away.

'Thank you. I thought for a moment that you were going to add that one to my other accomplishments. Liar, cheat, coward—they do add up, don't they?' She was hurting inside more than she liked to admit. For a few beautiful moments there had been no one but the three of them and she longed for him to reach out and take her hand again, but he didn't.

'Stop it, Olivia! I'm not in the mood to quarrel with you. I'm holding in my arms the wonderful gift you gave me and for the moment I'm at peace. Don't try to start a quarrel now.'

She kept silent, only looking at him as they paused outside her grandfather's room. She was afraid now that the shock would be too much for the old man, and her anxiety was in her eyes as she looked up into the dark face of the man who stood beside her.

'Don't worry, he's not about to scold you for giving him a great-grandson, and if you're thinking that the shock will kill him then you couldn't be more wrong.' His free hand came out to touch her face and for a second he smiled down at her. 'Come on, Olivia. Get a hold on those nerves.'

He opened the door and pushed her gently forward into the lamplit room.

'Grandfather.' Her voice sounded so unlike her own that she had to stop as the craggy old face turned to hers.

'Well, at last!' he grumbled. 'I've hardly seen you today. I thought you might come back again, but I can see it's too much trouble to come up twice to an old man.'

'Shut up, you old wretch! Olivia has been too busy and worried to keep coming up here to listen to your moaning.'

Andreas stepped into the room, Nicky nestled in his arms, and for a moment all other movement was arrested as the old man stared unbelievingly at the small dark head that rested so comfortably against the powerful shoulder of his father.

'Our son, Alex,' Andreas said softly as his arm came around Olivia's trembling shoulders. 'What did you want her to do, come to chatter at you, or bring you your great-grandson?'

Alex Skouradis uttered a single cry, half rising from his chair and then sinking back, his face white as driven snow.

'Grandfather!' Olivia's horrified cry as she hurried over to him seemed to bring him back to reality, and his still strong arms hugged her to him as she knelt beside his wheelchair.

'Olivia! Olivia!' He rocked her close, cradling her head as if she too were still the child he had cradled so long ago. 'Dry your eyes, child,' he murmured roughly. 'It's a miracle. A miracle you kept from me.' He held her away and looked into her eyes. 'Why, child? Why haven't I seen him before?'

'I—I was afraid of losing him. I'm sorry, Grandfather.'

'There, child, didn't I tell you that you were too

young? Didn't I tell you too?' He glared up at Andreas and then made an impatient gesture. 'Well, bring him here, bring him here.'

Nicky, half asleep and quite comfortable where he was, had no desire to be foisted off on to this old man with a voice like thunder and showed it in no uncertain terms, struggling fiercely to cling to Andreas and then, seeing Olivia, yelling at the top of his voice and demanding to be handed to Mummy.

'He's tired, Alex.' Andreas grinned widely as he handed the struggling bundle to Olivia. 'Your greetings will have to wait until morning. When this young man wants something, he wants it at once. Right now it's very obvious exactly what he wants.' His eyes were soft as they rested on Olivia, her son cradled to her breast with his chubby little arm around her neck and his thumb in his mouth, already drowsy again, his dark eyes closing.

'Beautiful, eh?' Andreas looked with proud challenging eyes towards Alex and the old man nodded, his eyes twinkling.

'Yes, beautiful, if you like that sort of thing. I would have preferred it had he been like my Olivia. Next time, eh? Next time a green-eyed imp for me. This one looks too much like his father—and sounds like him too.' He laughed softly and the two men looked with pride at the latest addition to the Skouradis clan.

Next time! What was he thinking of? He knew that downstairs her fiancé waited with ill-concealed annoyance for her return. He was talking as if she was still married to Andreas, as if everything was normal. True, he hadn't seen the desperate scene this morning when Andreas had gone off to fetch his son, to steal him from her, but he knew that she was going to marry Peter.

Olivia felt a burst of anger against him, against both of them. They were so filled with pride, so arrogant that the wishes of anyone else were totally discounted.

'I'm sorry, but it's way past his bedtime. I'll have to get him into bed. I'll bring him in the morning, Grandfather, there's no getting any sense out of him when he's so tired.'

She walked quickly to the door and Andreas followed her, calling to her grandfather that they would both be back later.

'I fed him on the flight,' he told her quietly as he trailed behind her towards her room. He seemed to be determined to keep his son in view, and she wondered rather crossly just what he thought she would be able to do to spirit Nicky away now that they were both prisoners.

'How did you manage that unlikely feat?' she asked grumpily.

'Automatic pilot, sandwiches, prepared by your Aunt Beth, and a certain innate skill that I seem to have been born with that enables me to tackle the unruly,' he informed her wryly.

'He's not unruly!' She glared at him as she went into her room, her lips tightening even more when he followed. 'He's just a tired little boy.'

'He was unruly long before he became tired,' Andreas insisted. 'That young man is very self-willed.'

'I suppose you're implying now that I'm not capable of looking after my own child?' Olivia put Nicky temporarily on her bed and he quickly curled into a ball and went to sleep.

'No. He seems to be in perfect condition.' He stared down in fascination at the sleeping little form. 'How beautiful he is!' He was silent and for the moment very grave as he watched his son. 'I expect he has inherited a temper from somewhere,' he added thoughtfully, and Olivia snorted crossly as she came from the bathroom where she had run warm water into the washbasin in readiness for the quick rub over that was all Nicky was going to get tonight in the way of a bath.

'I wonder where he got it from?' she asked sarcastically.

'You're very bad-tempered yourself at the moment, Olivia,' he observed as she bent over Nicky to remove his clothes. 'Isn't that going to wake him up?'

'No! He's too far gone to realise what's happening.'

She lifted the sleeping little boy and cuddled him to her as she walked back to the bathroom, and once again Andreas followed, coming right up to the washbasin and peering at them both with an expression of astonishment on his face as if the washing of a baby was some new and fascinating spectacle.

Everywhere she went he was one step behind her, handing her things she didn't want and hovering over his son, his eyes never leaving the sleeping little face.

'What do you want me to do next?' He regarded her solemnly as she tucked Nicky up in her bed, and she had to turn away as her sense of humour almost got the better of her. He hadn't done anything at all yet, except get in the way!

'Nothing—I've finished.'

'You can't leave him here! He'll roll on to the floor!' His voice rose and she shushed him impatiently.

'He'll be perfectly all right.' She put a pillow at each side of Nicky and prepared to walk out of the room, but Andreas was far from satisfied and hurriedly put a chair at each side of the bed.

'He can't sleep here all night. He needs a room and a bed of his own. I'll organise it immediately after dinner, then you can move him.' He sounded so self-satisfied that her temper rose again and she glared into his face.

'He has a bed of his own, but unfortunately, as you can well imagine, it's in England and therefore a little too far away!'

'Whatever you do, whatever you say, I'll not quarrel with you tonight, Olivia,' Andreas said quietly. 'I'm too happy.'

'I was happy—once.' She turned to the door, but he reached for her quickly, pulling her into his arms, his fingers threading through her hair as he held her head up to his.

'Perhaps, as you've had him for so long, you don't realise what he means to me.' He pulled her closer, his arm tightening around her, and she felt all the fight leaving her as she stood in the lamplight, her son sleeping peacefully close by, her body beginning to stir at the touch of the strong hands that held her. 'You were always extraordinary.' His eyes roamed over her face. 'Your fresh skin, your green eyes, your silken hair—I could never keep my eyes off you even when you were a child. Later I wanted to touch you all the time. Now you've performed a miracle. You've produced my son, and he's perfect.'

Olivia stirred, not wanting him to know how much she needed this, how much she needed his love, his strength, how much she needed to hand over all the doubts and responsibilities to him and lean against his strong hard chest.

'It's been hard, hasn't it, Olivia? Difficult to cope and look after my son while you determinedly worked to get him the things he needed.'

'Aunt Beth helped me.' There were tears in her eyes that she couldn't hide, and he murmured softly, treating her like she treated Nicky when he was hurt.

'My poor Olivia! You were so young. My poor little darling!'

'I don't want your pity!' she gasped, struggling in his arms. 'I managed without you. I did it all by myself!'

'You didn't do it all by yourself, *karithia mou*,' he said softly, his hand cupping her face. 'You gave me a beautiful baby, but I gave him to you first.'

His lips claimed hers as both his arms tightened round her and she couldn't resist the need to surrender.

Her arms lifted as if they had a life of their own, her fingers seeking the thick darkness of his hair.

With a low moan he pulled her close until she was moulded to the hard muscles of his body and his caressing hand slid beneath the hem of her shirt to stroke the soft curve of her spine.

She had to arch against him in rapture as his skilful fingers found every nerve ending, as his mouth opened over hers and devoured her sweetness. Moments ago they had been facing each other in this room and there had been anger in her heart, now she felt nothing but ecstasy, a burning need to stay in the enfolding warmth of his embrace, to move willingly with the hands that fondled her.

'Dear God, Olivia, I want you! I want you here and now!' The eyes that had been gentle and filled with tender pity were burning like hot coals as they held hers.

With one swift movement he pulled the soft shirt over her head and stared down at the thrusting beauty of her breasts, their arousal all the signal he needed.

'Don't tell me that you don't want this too, my beautiful witch,' he murmured, his hands moving with one sweeping caress from her shoulders to cover her breasts. He held her fast, his dark head bent to allow his lips to nuzzle against her, his teeth gently biting her heated flesh.

'Come with me, sweet, belong to me again. It's been so long, so very long.'

She was ready to do anything he asked and she clung to him unashamedly, welcoming his petting hands, cradling against him until his racing heart beat in time with her own and all his crimes were forgotten.

'Olivia!' His arms tightened to lift her and she knew that she would do anything he asked. This was Andreas, her whole life except for the small being he had created who slept in peace beside them.

All other things were forgotten as his lips possessed hers fiercely, and then they both heard Sophia calling, her voice getting nearer every second.

'Damn!' Andreas released her as he realised that they had left the door open, their need for each other so overwhelming that propriety seemed to have been forgotten.

He was at the door in a flash, giving Olivia time to recover, to pull her shirt on and tidy her hair.

'What is it, Sophia? We're putting Nicky to bed and you're all set to waken him.'

'I wanted to see him—Tomas told me. Andreas, I'm so happy!'

Olivia saw the tension leave his shoulders as he stepped into the corridor and closed the door.

'We all are, Tia Sophia. We need to set up a room for him next to this one. Perhaps you can help after dinner?'

She heard the happy murmur of Sophia's voice die away and she sank to the bed beside Nicky, her head in her hands. What had she done now? What had happened to her that she could let this madness grip her as soon as he touched her? Not one thing was changed. She was still engaged to Peter, and though she knew now that she could never go through with the marriage, that she could never marry anyone when she still loved Andreas, still she could not be so dishonourable as to go to Andreas when Peter was under the same roof.

She knew in her heart that had not Sophia appeared so fortuitously on the scene, she would have gone with him, and regretted it bitterly afterwards. He was still the same, softened perhaps by the magical discovery of his son, but still the same beneath it all.

She was not to have Leandi forced upon her, but she was still there, Olivia had few doubts about that. Even while she had been on the island, Andreas had disappeared, and where else would he be going? He had disappeared in a similar manner often in the past and left her anxious and waiting. If she stayed she would have to face that every day, and she could never face it, not even for Nicky. She wanted nothing from Andreas if she could not have his love.

Now that Nicky was discovered, she supposed her options were greater. There was nothing now to fear if Andreas followed her to London, but he would never let Nicky go. It was all he had ever wanted. And if he married again, could she bear the thought of Leandi Kastakis touching her son?

If anything, the difficulties were enhanced. There was now nothing that she could do, unless she could steal Nicky back, and was the world a big enough place in which to hide from Andreas?

She got up and brushed her hair. Dinner was ready, but she had neither the desire nor the energy to get changed. She looked at herself in the mirror, her soft tan shirt and skirt an unsuitable outfit for dinner in the splendour of the Skouradis dining room, but she shrugged wearily. It would have to do. With one last glance at Nicky's sleeping form, she went down to face Andreas.

He had not changed either. He was still wearing the dark blue shirt and grey trousers that he had left the house in that morning, his sleeves now rolled up to show his strongly muscled forearms.

He glanced at her, his lips twitching humorously, his dark eyes resting on Peter's face. Peter had changed.

'I wish you'd told me that no one else was going to dress for dinner, Olivia!' Peter hissed at her as they took their seats.

'We were too busy to change,' Andreas answered for her. 'I'm afraid we have been too wrapped up in settling our son to either bother to dress for dinner or to see to the requirements of our guest. Do not let it embarrass you, however, it is Olivia and I who are improperly dressed.'

His affable way of speaking startled Peter as much as it had startled Olivia and for a moment he was nonplussed. His social graces came to his rescue, however, and he managed a tight smile, clearly relieved that he was to be spoken to by his host on this occasion.

'No matter, I expect it's all been a bit of a surprise. A child can bring a great deal of turmoil into any household.'

'I expect we shall learn to cope.' Andreas smiled pleasantly and Olivia caught his eyes, frowning at his thinly veiled sarcasm. Peter did not know this type of man. Andreas was totally outside his experience, beyond his comprehension.

She looked sternly at Andreas and again his lips twitched in a wicked smile.

It seemed that every servant in the house was taking it in turns to serve at the table or come in on some excuse to look with delight and admiration at Olivia. She had produced an heir for her husband, for to them she was still Madame Skouradis, but more than that, she had produced his exact image and had made him completely happy. She was a woman without equal at the moment, and Olivia knew that her name would be on the lips of everyone in the village by morning.

Andreas met her eyes in a moment of understanding, his gaze sweeping over her with open possession, regardless of her fiancé sitting there, and she felt her anger begin to boil again. He thought he had won. He thought that he had put her neatly in her place, a wife to stay at home and raise his son, while he continued to live his life without interruption.

She looked away with tightened lips, and when she glanced up later, it was to meet the narrow-eyed speculation of the man who sat at the head of the table. She looked at him coolly and saw anger replace the gentle irony of his former looks. He had read her mind as usual. So much the better, it would save putting it into words.

She left the table at the end of the meal and hurried away, telling Peter that she had to see to Nicky, and in his new-found confidence as an accepted guest, he did not demur.

She was quickly overtaken by Andreas, however, who did not enquire why she had suddenly turned back into the ice-cold person who had greeted him in Athens. Instead, he informed her that a bed had been prepared for Nicky in the room next to hers and that she could move him now.

It was a small white room and she could see at once that this would make a lovely room for any child. She had almost forgotten about it, and marvelled that three years should have pushed from her mind so many things. There was a small bed already made up, its whitewood ends gaily decorated with small animals.

'Where did you get this from?' She forgot to be angry for the moment, and Andreas surveyed the bed and the room with satisfaction.

'It was the bed that your mother slept in as a child, and my mother too before her.' He had always called his new stepmother mother, and even though his father had gone to live in America years ago, he still kept in close touch with them. 'I discussed it with Sophia before dinner and she reminded me that there were such things in the attics. Tomas brought it down while we were eating. The mattress has always been kept aired.'

'Whatever for?' She fell into the trap neatly.

'For our children, Olivia. I sometimes think that we two were the last to know that we would marry.'

'Yes.' For one moment she sympathised with him. He had been given no more choice than she had. Without interference and the responsibilities of the business, he would have married Leandi.

'This room will make a good nursery, don't you

think?' He looked at her, his eyes meeting hers squarely, challenging her to deny him.

'Temporarily.' She said nothing more and after a moment he asked,

'Did you have some other place in mind?'

'Yes, of course I have. You don't imagine that Nicky is going to stay here indefinitely? When I take him back to England this bed can be put back into store.'

She smoothed the covers over Nicky and turned, to find herself grasped viciously by the arms.

'My son will never leave Greece!' Andreas' eyes were like fire, his lips one hard, straight line, and though she struggled and pulled, she could not get free.

'I have no intention of staying here, and when I go, Nicky goes too.' She knew that she was fighting without weapons, but the memory of her response to him before dinner drove her on to defy him, to establish some ground rules for the future.

'He stays. If you wish to leave, do so. Now that I have my son, I don't care what you do. If you are determined to marry that pompous friend of yours, then go ahead and marry him, but don't think that he will share my son or that you will ever see Nicky again!'

'I'll not let you keep Nicky. If you think I would stand by and see you marry Leandi Kastakis and hand Nicky over to her, then you're mistaken. I'd kill her!'

Olivia's own voice had risen and this time it was Andreas who shushed her as Nicky stirred restlessly. Andreas regarded her with sardonic amusement.

'Jealous, kitten?' he drawled softly. 'Jealous of her? Why? For Nicky, or for me?'

He caught the hand that shot up to slap his face, gripping her wrist and pulling her closer, laughing down into her face.

'Not two hours ago, you wanted me, *karithia mou.* Do you imagine that I have forgotten? Do you think I cannot still feel the body that was pressed so feverishly to mine? We can continue this fight in our old room if you wish, or do you prefer to go down and join your nice friend?'

'I hate you, and I'll get the better of you yet!' she spat out at him, her eyes flashing fire.

'You'll never get the better of me, my darling, unless you return to my bed, and as to hating me—you're a liar, and a very poor one. You want me as much as I want you, but you are not honest enough to admit it, you leave it to your body to speak for you. You will admit it though, Olivia, my little wildcat, you will admit it very soon.'

He released her wrist and turned to the door and just as she was relaxing, thinking that he was about to leave, he turned swiftly and caught her to him, kissing her startled mouth into submission before letting her go again.

'I could take you now,' he jeered, 'but never mind, go and entertain your fiancé. I'll see you tomorrow and we'll discuss our son.'

Furious and humiliated, Olvia stormed from the room and made for the stairs, the softly jeering laughter following her as Andreas went into his own room— their room. She had taken all she could take and she had one intention only, to get as near drunk as possible.

She found Peter in the dining room and he smiled benignly on her, rising at once to get her a drink when she made with determination towards the cabinet that housed the sherry. She wasn't used to drinking, but she quite liked the taste of sherry and that would do as well as anything for her purpose.

'He can be quite charming when he behaves himself.'

'Who?' Olivia regarded Peter in surprise. Surely he couldn't be talking about Andreas, not after the scene the other day when they had been all set to lay into each other. Men! Her grandfather was just as bad. And hadn't he noticed the sarcastic tone of the charm that had been poured on to him?

'Skouradis, of course, who else? I imagine that now he has Nicky he can afford to be charming, but I can tell you it's a relief to me. It's not very comfortable to stay in a house where you're not welcome, even your grandfather is very badly behaved, in my opinion.'

'Oh?' This was news. She didn't know he had seen her grandfather after the first introduction when Alex Skouradis had regarded Peter in sombre silence for fully ten seconds and then had burst out with one of his piratical laughs. That had been rude, she had to admit, but as far as she had known, Peter hadn't seen the old man since.

'He sent someone to find you when you'd gone off for that walk with that big gorilla of yours. When you couldn't be found, he sent for me. We talked for a while.'

'What about?' She held her glass out and he refilled it, frowning anxiously.

'Do you think you should, Olivia?'

She shook the glass under his nose and he filled it to the top. She was intrigued by her grandfather's call to him and annoyed to hear Tomas referred to as a gorilla. At this moment he was the only decent man in the world.

'What about?' she repeated stubbornly and he sat down with an exaggerated sigh, but not before putting the sherry well out of the way.

'Oh, this and that, you know. I told him that you were upset because Skouradis had gone off to get Nicky.'

'You what!' She was furious. Furious with Peter for telling her grandfather and furious with the old man for pretending such heartbreaking shock. At that moment she would have liked to tie Peter, Andreas and her grandfather together and push them off the cliff.

'Well, I mean he was bound to know before nightfall. It wasn't a secret any longer, Olivia, and I thought it would make a talking point. He's a difficult old devil to talk to.'

'There's a knack to it,' Olivia said with perfect calm. 'You just keep quiet and let him talk, he's very good at it.'

'Well, he did talk, at some length,' Peter conceded. 'I had to agree with him, of course, when he said that Nicky's place was here. You know my thoughts on that subject, Olivia.'

'I do, I do.' She suddenly felt very solemn and calm, and made her way determinedly to the sherry, shaking her head firmly at Peter when he intervened.

'Now then, Peter, this is my home and my sherry,' she remonstrated seriously. 'You shouldn't interfere with a person in their own home with their own sherry.'

She couldn't understand why he was looking at her strangely, it was a perfectly logical thing to say, and she held her glass steady as she refilled it. They were big glasses, she wasn't quite sure if they were sherry glasses—still, what did it matter, they were very nice glasses. She began to giggle at the thought, though why she wasn't sure, and Peter stood abruptly, coming across to her and taking her arm.

'You're just a little drunk, I think, Olivia,' he said grimly. 'I'll take you to bed before you make a fool of yourself.'

'Thank you—no.' She knew it was necessary to behave with dignity. 'Andreas has already offered to take me to bed, but I declined. I can't accept your offer either, Peter. You can go up, though, I expect you're tired. It's been an exciting day for you.'

He stood looking at her for a few seconds, he seemed quite angry about something and she imagined just for a moment that he was swaying a little, though it might have been her.

'Off you go then, dear,' she said brightly, and after one last exasperated glance at her, he went.

It seemed to Olivia that someone was lifting her and she was grumbling about it because she was so comfy. Someone was laughing too, laughing so softly that she almost missed it. She started to laugh too, and then she was stopped by the simple expedient of having her face turned into somebody's shoulder.

She grumbled at that, but a voice told her that she would wake Nicky and she knew not to do that. Nicky must not be disturbed, she said solemnly, and there was somebody agreeing with her very seriously.

She was cold for a minute and then soft bedclothes were being pulled over her, stopping at her waist while lips kissed her breasts. That wasn't right, she started to say so, but was told that it was perfectly all right, and after a while she agreed, even feeling disappointed when the bedclothes were pulled to her chin and nobody was there any more.

She awoke later in the night with such a terrible headache that for a few moments she dared not move her head. She finally managed to struggle up in bed and switch on the light. Three o'clock! She felt sick and ill, and there was some sort of message on a big white card by the clock.

She grabbed it as she raced for the bathroom, and after a few minutes of agony she was able to screw up her eyes sufficiently to be able to read it.

It was big writing. Obviously somebody knew how sherry affected the optic nerve.

'The aspirin are in the cabinet. You were out cold, try a cold wet compress. Andreas. P.S. You're still beautiful.'

She stared at the note in shocked disbelief and then looked down at her shivering body. She hadn't a stitch of clothing on. The somebody she had vaguely felt carrying her to bed had been Andreas. At this moment she was too relieved to know that he had put aspirin in the cabinet to feel anything else. She would feel all that was expected of her in the morning, she knew that.

Right now, she needed to get back into her bed, and after swallowing two aspirin, she staggered back to her room and fell into bed, pulling the sheets over her with a moan of pain.

'That will teach you to lay off the hard stuff, my girl,' she groaned, thankful that sleep was already beginning to claim her.

Her last waking thoughts were strange. She was glad that it hadn't been Peter. Somebody had laughed at her and kissed her, Peter would never have done that. Peter would have been very angry and embarrassed, but Andreas had laughed. What a pity he didn't love her.

She started to cry softly, all the misery of the days without him building up and flooding out on to her pillow. She had imagined herself free, but now it seemed that she had merely been holding her breath, waiting in a dismal world to find Andreas again. It was terrible to be in love with someone who loved somebody else. There would be no other children, no other babies who looked like Andreas, not for her anyway.

She would have to tell Peter, and she debated in her pain filled, muddled mind whether to tell him at once or wait until they returned to England. She didn't wish to cause him any humiliation and she felt uneasy now about him. He had shown himself to be quite capable of causing a scene. Her mother had once said wisely that you never really knew someone until you saw them in their own background, but Olivia was beginning to think that perhaps the reverse was also true. She had discovered here a side to Peter's nature that she had never suspected, unless she had been deliberately blinding herself to it.

She had found him to be selfish in many small ways,

and with regard to Nicky and her own love for her son, Peter had been quite unfeeling. He had discovered a way to get rid of the unwelcome intrusion into his life of another man's son and she knew he would play it for all it was worth. If he could be like that, he didn't love her either.

The thought brought more tears and she fell asleep filled with remorse, guilt and the certainty that her unhappiness would last for ever.

CHAPTER SEVEN

Next morning, Olivia was still suffering. She lay in bed, her head throbbing, trying to go over the events of the previous evening, but finally giving up and rolling on to her side with a groan of self-pity.

The sound of Nicky's laughter had her sitting up quickly a few minutes later and she glanced at the clock, noticing with a feeling of guilt that it was already nine. She couldn't remember when she had last stayed in bed so late. Nicky was an early riser and saw to it that everyone else got up too.

She slipped into her robe and went to the balcony, looking down at the swimming pool that was almost directly under her window. The sound of laughter had come from somewhere here, but for the moment the glare of the sunlight on the clear water of the pool blinded her to everything else and increased the throbbing in her head.

Then she saw Nicky. He was toddling along beside the pool, looking back over his shoulder, his unsteady gait taking him closer to the glittering water with every step, and from her position above the scene, it seemed to Olivia that at any moment he would fall into the pool.

In her mind she could already see him falling, the clear, deep water closing around his head. She was so far away. It would have happened long before she could race down the stairs and save him.

She began to scream his name, realising as she did that it was entirely the wrong thing to do, for the little head lifted to find the source of her voice and his legs wobbled even more. Even so she couldn't seem to stop screaming out to him, and her cries were not silenced when two strong brown arms shot out and lifted Nicky into the air.

'Olivia!' Andreas was looking up at her, shouting to her, but her hysterical screams were still continuing.

'Olivia!' he roared like a bull, and she was silent, leaning over the rail of the balcony, her face white, her legs only just supporting her. 'Get away from the rail! Get back into the bedroom! Do you hear me, Olivia— get back!' His roaring began to penetrate her mind and she staggered back out of sight, belatedly aware that she had been hanging over the rail on the point of imbalance, in almost as much danger as she had imagined for Nicky.

She was not halfway across the room before Andreas burst in, Nicky in his arms, his face pale and angry.

'You little fool! You almost fell! What did you think was happening? Do you imagine that I would let my son go wandering off beside the pool alone? Someone is beside him almost every step he takes.' His anger began to fade as he saw the condition that she was in, her face now what she imagined would be a pale shade of green as nausea washed over her. A shock on top of a hangover was not a good mixture. With a groan of pain she sank to the nearest chair, cradling her head in her hands.

'Pretty bad, is it?' She glanced up, expecting to see a glint of sarcasm in his eyes, but he was smiling sympathetically, so she nodded, regretting it at once as her head threatened to detach itself from her body.

'Stay there a minute. Can you just keep an eye on Nicky?' He put Nicky to the floor and she still found the strength to glare at him.

'I've been taking care of him for the last two years, I think I can manage a minute.'

'You'll have help from now on.' He strode over to

the window and closed it before making for the door.
'We'll close you in, just in case.'

He was gone before she could think of a reply and
she heard his steps hurrying along the passage and
taking the stairs two at a time. It came to something
when she couldn't be trusted to look after her own son
for two minutes! She couldn't even summon up the
energy to pick him up, and for once he was silent,
looking at her with great solemn brown eyes, standing
exactly where Andreas had left him, as if he was under
strict orders not to move.

Andreas was back in what seemed like two seconds, a
glass of disgusting-looking liquid in his hand that Olivia
eyed fearfully.

'What's that?' Her tormented stomach began to
protest at the very sight of it, but he advanced on her
steadily, his face determined, and she knew she was
going to drink it, although it looked more like
something that should be rubbed into the back for
aches and pains.

'Old remedy for a hangover.' He stood over her and
held out the glass, putting it firmly in her trembling
hands when she made no attempt to take it. 'This will
have you on your feet in a few minutes.'

'What's in it?' She grimaced into the murky liquid,
the contents of the glass a sickening shade of brown.

'Secret potion—everything from the kitchen. Down
the hatch!

He picked Nicky up and settled him on his arm, both
of them staring at her like doctors without hope.

'I—I don't think I can. I'm too sick, I . . .' Olivia looked
forlornly at them, but they weren't giving ground.

'Hatch,' said Nicky, and Andreas nodded.

'Right now!' he agreed.

They were watching her closely, both with the same
dark-eyed determination, like grim-looking twins, two
males who would give no quarter, and she closed her

eyes and swallowed the foul-looking mixture. If it killed her then at least she would be out of her misery.

It hit her like an explosion, setting fire to her throat and then to her stomach, and her eyes looked wildly up at Andreas to find him grinning widely.

For a moment she didn't know whether to run for the bathroom or race round the room like a cat with its fur on fire, but before she could decide which to do, the unexpected happened—she felt fine. The dazzling coloured lights that had been in front of her eyes ever since she opened them faded away, her stomach returned to normal and the day looked decidedly brighter.

'Magic!' She stared at Andreas and he nodded with satisfaction.

'It never fails. You'll be all right now, and as you're so sure that Nicky is going to be allowed to drown, you can come and help me to give him his first swimming lesson.'

'Has he been fed?' She knew it was a silly question, Nicky demanded food as soon as his eyes were open. This contented child who sat proudly on his father's arm had certainly been fed.

'Hours ago—you were still asleep. Sophia and I managed. You can wait for your breakfast until we've been in the pool. The mixture will hold you for now.'

'I suppose you're an expert on hangovers?' Olivia ventured with a return to the offensive now that she had her own head back.

'Yes, but never my own. I like to keep my wits about me.' He shot her a sideways glance filled with mockery. 'You had few wits last night, Olivia. You could have been in big trouble, allowing yourself to be so vulnerable.'

'Thank you for looking after me.' She felt very ashamed of herself, her face flooding with colour as she avoided his penetrating gaze.

'In many ways, it was a pleasure,' he conceded softly, 'but you were just a little bit over the top.'

She didn't want to be reminded about last night, the realisation that she was wearing nothing under her thin robe embarrassing her even further.

'About that swim——' Andreas obviously intended to drop the subject of her venture into alcoholism, but her tongue just kept on going.

'I thought you had to have "the hair of the dog that bit you"?'

'Only if you're a practised drunk. You're merely an amateur. I trust you do not intend to put in any further practice?'

'No,' she looked away rapidly at the sight of his raised eyebrows, 'I—I can't come for a swim. I didn't bring a swimsuit with me, in fact I haven't got one at all.'

She had never swum since she had left Illyaros and she had been longing to get into the pool or go down to the sea for the past two days.

'Come along then. We should be able to remedy that too.' Andreas marched out of the room carrying Nicky, and she followed like a slave trailing along behind the master.

He flung open the door of the bedroom that she had never entered since her return to the island—their bedroom—and when she hesitated in the doorway he shot her an exasperated glance.

'You're quite safe. We have a chaperon.'

He bent to the chest of drawers where her clothes used to be, and Olivia gasped as she saw that they were still there, in perfect order. Delicate lacy undies, things she could not afford now, neat piles of slips and panties that had cost a fortune. She came forward slowly, her eyes startled, her mouth almost watering at the sight of so much luxury.

There were costumes too, brief bikinis in brilliant colours, everything just where she had left them.

'You—you kept them?' She glanced up at him, not knowing whether to be embarrassed that they were both staring down at brief silky panties, or delighted that they were still there.

'Obviously!' Andreas frowned at her and turned away, poking among the swim wear. 'There should be something here to suit you for the moment.' He pulled out a bright red top and searched for the other piece. 'What about this?'

It had always been his favourite, and she couldn't make up her mind whether to be happy or miserable that he had homed in on that at once.

'I doubt if it will fit. I—I'm bigger than I was.' Olivia blushed at his burst of laughter and looked anywhere but into his eyes.

'Only in the right places, Olivia,' he assured her softly. 'After last night I can vouch for that.'

'Olivia!'

The voice was so sharp, so unexpected and so condemning that Olivia actually jumped guiltily as they both turned to see Peter standing in the doorway of the room, his face furious and red.

'What are you doing in this room?' She felt a guilt that was completely without justification. The door had been wide open, Nicky was bouncing noisily on the huge double bed and though she was wearing only her robe, it did cover her completely. For a second she could think of no reply, but Andreas had no such inhibitions.

'My wife is getting herself a swimsuit. Her clothes are here. Would you like to see them?' He was angry, she could tell that. He strode across the room and slid open the long white wardrobe that almost filled one wall. 'These belong to Olivia, and they are naturally in our room. Where else would you expect them to be?' He stood aside, and Peter's eyes widened at the sight of the rows of expensive dresses, suits and evening gowns that

hung neatly on the rails. He had kept them all, and
suddenly she forgot about Peter, her eyes on Andreas
who for some reason would not meet her startled gaze.

'Er ... quite. Er ... sorry, you startled me for a
moment. I—I'll see you downstairs, Olivia.'

He never enquired how she felt, although he knew
that she normally never stayed in bed for so long, he
didn't even apologise to her. His apologies had been
directed towards Andreas, and as he went off down the
stairs Olivia glanced sideways at the tall angry figure
beside her. He was fuming.

'You kept all my clothes?' She didn't know what to
say really, and he looked down at her darkly, his eyes
inscrutable.

'There's some sentimentality in the best of us, Olivia.'
He thrust the bikini into her hands and began to walk
out of the room. 'Try that. If it doesn't meet with your
approval then you know where the rest are.' He was
gone before she could tell him that Nicky had no
swimsuit either, though she expected that he had
realised this and was prepared to deal with it.

He did. When she arrived at the pool, slender and
self-conscious in the red bikini, it was to find that
Andreas and Nicky were already in the water, and a
very bored Peter was sitting on a lounger as far away
from them as conditions would permit.

Andreas had changed into brief black shorts in the
little room beside the pool where there were always
towels and where he usually changed. Nicky was
bouncing delightedly in strong brown arms, his
swimming apparel the shorts he had been wearing, only
his little shirt discarded by the edge of the pool.

'Come in and help me.' His anger cast aside,
Andreas grinned up at her, his eyes narrowed against
the glare, but still brilliantly alive as he inspected her
slim figure.

'I told you it would fit. It looks better than ever.'

Peter liked this little, and the wide grin widened further as Andreas glanced at him.

'This is a two-man job. Get your bikini wet, Olivia, before I decide to come out and get you.'

She slid into the water, sensuously aware of the silkiness of her skin as the pool closed over her, aware too of the scant covering of both herself and Andreas as she surfaced close by and reached for Nicky.

They played with him for twenty minutes, his delight in the water pleasing Andreas, his antics amusing them until the pool rang with laughter, and Alex appeared on his balcony shouting instructions which they ignored and threatening to come downstairs to join in.

When at last Andreas declared that they had all had enough, Olivia realised with a shock that for the past twenty minutes she had been completely happy, happier than she had been for the last three years. She realised too, with some guilt, that she had completely forgotten about Peter, and catching his disapproving stare, she knew that he had noticed the fact.

'Enough, young man!' Andreas scooped Nicky from the pool, to be instantly choked by two wet, clinging arms.

'Kiss me! Kiss me!' demanded Nicky urgently, and Andreas obliged before turning mocking eyes on Olivia.

'Now where does he get this frantic desire to be kissed from, do you imagine?'

'It's—it's only his way,' she answered shakily, avoiding his amused glance, horrified at her own desire to be held in those strong arms still gleaming with water from the pool. He held Nicky so securely and she wanted him to reach out and hold her.

'I'm sure it is.' He regarded her slowly, his eyes on the full tight breasts that were only just concealed by the bikini top. He raised his eyes and held her gaze, his glance suddenly soft and warm.

'Did you enjoy your swim?' His quiet question

seemed to be not the thing that was on his mind at the moment and she could not answer, being too occupied with her own feelings and the overwhelming desire to simply look at him. It was almost impossible to keep her eyes from that strong brown body, the long powerful legs. He had always been superb. There had always been something extra about him that had drawn female glances wherever he went.

They were ignoring Peter, behaving as if there was nobody else in the world, and his eyes lingered over the slim perfection of her legs before locking with hers as his mouth tilted in a wicked smile.

'Do you want a cuddle too—from your energetic son?'

He handed Nicky to her with a low laugh, walking off to change as she hid her hot face in the cool, wet skin of the child. Andreas' ability to know what was in her mind was a dangerous capability. She would have to watch herself carefully in future. Just because he was delighted with Nicky, just because he had been gentle and kind, helping her when she needed him and joining in the play as if they were a happy family, it did not mean things had changed.

Discovering that she still loved him altered nothing at all. He did not love her, except as an interesting, desirable toy.

Naturally enough, now that Nicky was present, much of her time was taken up with him, and equally naturally, as his father, Andreas joined in, leaving aside whatever else he would normally have been doing to get to know his son and understand the mysteries of bringing up a small energetic boy.

Peter was left more to himself than Olivia would have wanted. Even with her change of heart she hated to neglect him—he was after all in the house of a stranger, and though she now had no desire to become his wife, she still felt a certain amount of gratitude towards him and affection for him.

He did not, however, relish being involved with a child, and as Nicky had to come first, Peter was left alone for the greater part of the day, a fact that Andreas seemed to note with grim satisfaction.

Olivia found that she held no resentment for Andreas in the matter of his son. His delight was infectious and she still found his eyes on her from time to time, looking at her as though she had produced a miracle that any other woman would have been incapable of producing.

She looked up at bathtime to see Andreas standing in the doorway, his eyes just a little wistful as he observed the hilarity and the pools of water on the floor. He made no move to enter, and she knew that he felt for the first time somewhat of an intruder.

'Do you want to help?' she asked hesitantly.

'What shall I do?' He came in, trying to conceal his eagerness, his eyes drawn to the front of her wet blouse, almost transparent now after the water that Nicky had splashed on her.

Olivia stood and reached quickly for a towel, draping it round her shoulders and avoiding his serious eyes.

'If it moves—wash it. I'll get into something dry. It's going to be your turn next, I warn you.'

He grinned and pulled his shirt off, dropping it on to the bathroom stool and crouching down beside the bath.

'That, I think, will even the odds. Pity you can't do that.' Olivia blushed and walked out, leaving him to cope, anxious to get away before her hands reached of their own free will to touch the smooth brown shoulders.

She could hear the squeals of laughter as she quickly discarded her wet clothes and slipped into her dressing gown, and later as she dried her freshly washed hair, she heard Sophia's happy murmurings as she mopped up the water, another willing slave to the two dark-eyed males in Olivia's life.

'What shall I do with him now?' Andreas tapped on her door and then walked in, Nicky wrapped securely in a towel, no escape possible.

'I'll dress him for bed and then give him some supper.' Olivia reached for Nicky and for a moment her hands became entangled with the strength of the brown hands that held her son. She looked at Andreas and would have taken Nicky, but he held on, his hands covering hers.

'I haven't thanked you today for my beautiful son,' he said softly. 'I never expected to be so happy again.'

What did he mean—again? She looked up into his night-black eyes, feeling like a besotted fool, but unable to look away, unwilling to break the spell.

Suddenly he released her hands and folded them both in his arms, his lips seeking hers in a kiss so sweet that she stood completely still, her eyes closed, her lips willingly clinging to his.

She opened her eyes when at last he released her and stared at him in captivated bewilderment. For a second neither of them spoke or moved, then Nicky wriggled and laughed.

'Nice kisses,' he observed, and Andreas looked at him with a grin.

'My sentiments precisely,' he admitted, and left them to get on with the struggle alone.

He was there in the kitchen when Olivia went down to feed Nicky, his eyes approving that she had not discarded her dressing gown. Somehow it added to the domesticity of the scene, and she put Nicky into his plastic coverall that Aunt Beth had so thoughtfully sent along and took the warm milky cereal from Sophia.

'How about this, then?' Andreas pulled forward a highchair from the darkened corner of the kitchen, watching Olivia's face as she looked at him in astonishment.

'From the attic?'

'From the attic,' he agreed. 'I saw you struggle with him at lunchtime and thought of balancing him on a few telephone directories, but Tomas and I made another sortie into the attics and found this.'

'It's lovely,' Olivia said, her eyes on the old, beautifully carved baby chair.

'It's childproof,' Andreas corrected, taking Nicky and fastening him in securely. 'Though perhaps not monsterproof,' he added thoughtfully.

Olivia didn't mind him calling Nicky a monster now that she could see how much he loved him. After all, she had called him that herself many times. She bit her lip and bent to feed him. Her mind was always slipping into the complacent feeling that this was for ever. It wasn't, and she would do well to remember that.

'Let me.' Andreas took the dish and crouched down beside Nicky, handing him the spoon, and she hadn't time to warn him before the sweet warm mush was plastered over his cheek as Nicky reverted to monsterism and wiped the spoon down his father's astonished face.

'I see.' Two dark eyes looked thoughtfully into two other dark eyes as both Olivia and Sophia stifled their laughter.

'If those are the rules then I will have to play by them.' Andreas took the spoon and calmly and deliberately returned the compliment, watching with interest as the little face registered first astonishment and then rage, the small chubby hand coming to test the side of his face where, like his father, a trickle of sweet liquid slid down his cheek.

For a second he glared at Andreas, fury in the dark beautiful eyes, and then he reached for the spoon and quietly got on with his supper.

'His father's son,' Andreas observed quietly, standing and wiping first his own face and then Nicky's. 'But as yet not big enough to win. What do you think, Sophia?'

Sophia nodded vigorously, her face still wreathed in laughter. 'A Skouradis if ever I saw one,' she agreed.

Olivia was still laughing too and Andreas turned to her, his head tilted at a teasing angle.

'Sherry, Olivia?' he enquired softly, his laughter following her as she fled to her room.

With Nicky finally tucked up in bed, Olivia prepared for dinner at leisure. She would not make the mistake tonight of failing to dress for dinner. Andreas too, she knew, would have reverted to his normally immaculate ways, especially after the wet and then sticky encounters with his son.

She put on the only other long dress she had brought with her, a pale, coffee-coloured chiffon, full-skirted and tight-waisted. It made her look very young, she thought uneasily, and she decided she had better leave her hair falling free, it would look strange piled up on her head in a dress like this.

She would have liked to go into the other bedroom and try on some of the beautiful gowns that were still there, but nothing would have persuaded her to do that. Safety lay a long way from Andreas and she would really be asking for trouble if she ventured into his room in her present state of mind.

She joined Andreas and Peter downstairs and was instantly aware that her flowing silky hair pleased Andreas and met with a frown of disapproval from Peter. She should have put it up, she thought crossly. Andreas liked it like this, it had always been a temptation to his fingers, and the fact that it made her feel young also added to the feeling of vulnerability that threatened to overwhelm her tonight.

For a whole day she had rarely been away from Andreas, and his warmth and gentleness had been constant. Of course she knew that she had Nicky to thank for this, but it was so easy to slip into the past, so easy to imagine that he loved her and wanted her because he loved her. To remind herself of Leandi was becoming a necessity with every hour that passed. He wanted to keep her here for his pride and to raise his son, but she felt herself being drawn under his spell as if she was at the other end of a magnet, slowly and inexorably being drawn into the circle of enchantment.

Peter was restless throughout dinner, as silent tonight as Andreas had been before he had discovered his son. There was a brooding air about the fair-haired man that finally registered with Olivia, and she wasn't somehow surprised when he threw his small bombshell.

'I think, my dear, that now you have your affairs more or less settled we should be going home, don't you?' Peter looked at her pleasantly, only the hard glitter of his eyes betraying his distaste for their present situation. 'I realise that you planned to stay longer, but there's so much to do when we get back. I've got two big cases to sort out and there's counsel to brief for another. If we're going to get time for a honeymoon we should make up the time before the wedding. It's very close now.'

He waited for her reply. He clearly had no idea that she had decided to call off the marriage as soon as they reached England. Of course neither had Andreas, in this he had not managed to read her mind.

The silence that followed Peter's lengthy statement was bristling with emotion—annoyance and distaste from Peter, distress and misery from Olivia and a waiting black silence from Andreas as he sat perfectly still at the head of the table, his eyes on her face.

If he had said something, given her any clue that he would be happy for her to stay for her own sake, Olivia would have answered differently. But he simply waited, his face still and cold, his eyes boring into her until she could feel her skin burning.

His fury was evident. She was his possession, the

mother of the small boy who had captured his heart. Her place was here, to raise his son, to make it clear to everyone that their separation had merely been the hysteria of an adolescent.

Damn you, Andreas! The words tore through her so strongly that she thought he must hear them. Go back to Leandi Kastakis, if you ever left her. Somehow I'll steal Nicky back. I'll take him with me when I go, then you can suffer too!

'You're probably right, Peter,' she said calmly. 'What about the day after tomorrow?'

'Perfect!' he smiled at her with a mixture of relief and tolerance. 'You're always such a sensible girl. Besides, you have all the details of the cases in that pretty little head.'

She didn't like to be spoken to like that, as if she was a halfwit, but she smiled, as close to simpering as she could manage, wondering why she felt suddenly empty and lost when Andreas stood abruptly and left the room.

She was on her way up the stairs when he caught her later, taking her arm and hauling her back into the study, closing the heavy door against prying eyes.

'So you're leaving? You're going to go back and marry that cold-blooded buffoon?'

He shook her as she struggled in his painful grasp and she fell silent and still. There was nothing she could do.

'Doesn't it mean anything to you, Olivia, that this is your home? Do you totally disregard your son, and Alex? I know you hate me, but I'm not the only one who lives here.'

She stared at the carpet, unable to raise her eyes. Hate him? She adored him, worshipped him. How did he imagine she could live here day after day and see him unless he loved her too?

'I have a future of my own,' she said defiantly. 'I was

getting along quite happily until Grandfather called me back to Greece. Now I'm going to take up my life again. What else did you think I would do?'

'You unnatural little bitch! What about your son?'

'I'm taking him with me!' She glared at him, anger her only refuge, and he tightened his grip, his eyes triumphant.

'Like hell you are, Olivia. You know that nothing will get Nicky away from me now. Go, and you lose him for ever.'

'Peter's a good solicitor, he'll help me,' she cried, gasping with pain as he gripped her arms. 'The law won't let you do this.'

'Won't it?' he sneered. 'Wait and see, Olivia, wait and see. Justice isn't at all what you imagine it to be—and as to your precious fiancé helping, don't imagine that I have failed to notice the looks of distaste he throws at our son. No other man will share my son.'

'But you're willing to let another woman share my son!' Olivia cried.

'When you marry that pompous jellyfish you'll find that he wields more authority with you than you imagine is in him. He is biding his time, my little fool. Once you're his wife you'll toe the line as you never were expected to toe it with me. He'll crush your spirit, but he'll not get the chance to crush Nicky. In my house I'll always be master, and I'll never be lenient with anyone as I have been with you. If Nicky should ever get a new mother, he will remain first and foremost my son.'

'He's mine too!' she cried, pictures of Leandi racing through her head, but he smiled cruelly.

'Not when you go, Olivia, never after you leave us. No law will take Nicky from me. Fortune smiles on the brave, they say, but it smiles more widely on millions and I would spend all I have to keep my son. I can battle with you until he is a grown man and you will still not have won. I'll make it my business to see that you never set eyes on him again.'

She tore from his grasp and ran from the room, tears streaming down her face. He meant it, she had no doubts about that. He wanted everything as usual, Nicky, herself and Leandi Kastakis.

Somehow she must get Nicky away. She would stay when Peter left and then bide her time. She could sail a boat as well as any man, Andreas had seen to that. She would lull him into a feeling of false security and then she would run, hide, take Nicky into hiding and never come out.

These desperate and unlikely thoughts were whirling around in her mind when Peter knocked on her door.

'I want to talk to you, Olivia.' He stood grimly outside, his eyes on her tear-stained face, and she motioned him into the room.

'What were you doing in the study with Skouradis?' He turned to her aggressively and began without preamble to put her severely in her place. 'I imagined that when you left the table you were on your way to see to the boy. I didn't for one moment think that you were sneaking off into the study to have a quiet word with Skouradis.'

On top of everything else, this was altogether too much, and Olivia began to seethe quietly. She looked at his thinned lips and angry face, and wondered what had happened to her mind that she had ever felt that Peter was quiet and easygoing, a rock to lean on. It seemed that Andreas was right, he was more like a rock to roll over and crush her.

'We were talking about Nicky.' She kept her voice quiet, and he stared at her closely.

'I can believe that, seeing the hysterics you seem to be indulging in. Good God, Olivia, the boy's not about to be killed! He's got everything going for him here. It's the best possible thing that could have happened to him. You should put his future first for a change instead of being so mollycoddling.'

'You never really wanted Nicky, did you, Peter?' Olivia faced him squarely and he looked a little put out.

'Olivia! You know I would have been happy to have given the boy a home with us.'

'Thank you, but I don't think being "given a home" is really what I wanted for Nicky.' If he called Nicky "the boy" just once more, she would scream!

'What do you mean by that exactly?' There was a certain mean look about his eyes, and Olivia was glad that the door was open. Not that she expected violence from Peter, but he was unlikely to rave when the whole household would hear.

'I think ...' she paused, uncertain as to how to continue. 'I'm going to have to stay here, Peter,' she went on in a rush. 'Andreas is keeping Nicky and I'll not leave without him. Anyway, I can't marry you. I couldn't marry you when I know that Nicky would always be there between us. I love him too much. Maybe you're right, maybe I am a little neurotic about him, but that's how it is.'

There was a moment of astonished silence and then Peter let out an exasperated sigh and walked forward to take her shoulders in a firm grasp.

'Now then, Olivia. You're letting things run away with you as usual. I can't think what's got into you since we've been here. You're quite a different person. Of course we're going to get married, it's all arranged and it will be a very suitable marriage too. We can discuss Nicky in more detail when we're back home and you can look at things with a better sense of perspective.'

He pushed the ring she had been removing back on to her finger.

'Let's have no more nonsense now. Get a good

night's sleep. Maybe we should go home tomorrow instead of waiting another day.'

He gave her a quick peck on the cheek and moved to the door, his arm still around her shoulders, both of them startled to see Andreas standing there, his face white with fury.

'Continue,' he bit out savagely. 'You must pardon my intrusion.'

'Just having a quiet word with Olivia.' Peter's face was a little red, but there was a certain satisfaction in his voice. 'Did you want to speak to her?'

'Not now.' Andreas looked at Olivia with burning anger. 'Anything that I had to say to Olivia is now of no importance. We seem to know where we stand after all.'

He turned and strode into the masters' bedroom, slamming the door with a finality that echoed through every part of Olivia's being.

CHAPTER EIGHT

SLEEP would be an impossibility, Olivia knew, and she was right. At midnight she was still tossing restlessly in her bed. Three times she had been in to look at Nicky for no real reason. Once asleep it was very rare indeed that he would wake up until morning and the need to eat stirred him into action.

Andreas would not spirit him away, why should he? Nicky was in the stronghold, the fortress, it was Olivia who would have to move him secretly, Andreas had no fear that she would be a threat to him in his desire to keep his son.

It was not Nicky who drew her from her bed, kept her from sleep, and she was well aware of the fact, although unwilling to face it. It was Andreas. She needed to be with him, longed for the last three years of her life to have been a long and unending nightmare. Longed to wake from her misery and find that she was still with Andreas, still his wife, still able to see the tender love on his face that she had once imagined shone there.

It was hot, with the closeness of imminent thunder in the air, and she wished that the threatened storm would come, anything to break this slow build-up of tension, this crazed longing that threatened to drive her mad.

Unable to bear the confines of her room any longer, she crept to the door and down the stairs to the kitchen in search of iced water or lemonade. Sophia always kept a supply of homemade lemonade in the fridge, and the heat made the prospect seem as tempting as her anger had made the sherry tempting on the previous night.

There were always dim lights left burning in the hall

and making her way to the kitchen quietly was not difficult. It was cooler there, the hard shining tiles of the floor an unusual comfort to her bare feet, and the iced lemonade was there, waiting for her in the huge earthenware jug at the back of the fridge, just as it had always been there since she was a child.

She filled her glass and leaned against the table in the middle of the kitchen, trying with all her might to make her mind a blissful blank. To banish Andreas from her waking thoughts in a way that he could never be banished from her dreams.

Empty glass still in her hand, she stared at the opposite wall attempting to mesmerise herself into a blank state of mind that would protect her from misery, when the sudden opening of the door shattered her calm, making her jump wildly and drop the tumbler. It fell to the tiles and broke on impact, scattering sharp dangerous pieces around her feet.

'Stand still!' The commanding voice kept her rooted to the spot, and Andreas strode into the kitchen, stepping across the broken glass and swinging her effortlessly up on to the table.

'Are you cut anywhere?' He ran his hands lightly down her ankles and across the soles of her bare feet, his grunt of relief and impatience telling her clearly that she was still intact.

'What are you doing, creeping about the house without slippers? Don't you have any slippers, either?' He looked at her with ill-concealed dislike, his brows drawn together in a black frown.

'Stay where you are.' He did not wait for her reply but cast a warning look at her that told her of the dire consequences of moving from her place on the table top at this moment.

'Where the devil does Sophia keep the brush?' He was crouching down beside the long bank of cupboards, opening and closing doors with mounting frustration, and Olivia dared a reply.

'End cupboard, bottom shelf.'

With an exclamation of satisfaction, he found it and reached into the back of the cupboard for the matching dustpan.

'I—I don't suppose you've ever used a brush and dustpan in your life before,' Olivia ventured shakily. She didn't know either what to do or say. It was longing for Andreas that had driven her from her room, but she had thought he was in bed and asleep hours ago. Yet here he was, dressed in the dark trousers of his suit that he had worn at dinner, the ruffled silk front of his shirt pulled impatiently open, his immaculate hair untidy as if he had been running his hands through it.

'No, I never have.' Still crouching, he appeared to give her slightly inane remark serious consideration. 'However, I'm sure that I grasp the general mechanics of the procedure.'

He stood and moved purposefully towards the broken glass, his face strained, and she wondered sadly what business deals had put the strain on his face this time. Once again she had no right to ask, no right to help.

He crouched at her feet, his capable hands wielding the brush as he gathered all the broken glass together, squinting sideways in the light to find the tiniest pieces, and Olivia stared down at the bent head, at the shining black hair, a need to touch him causing her throat to constrict, her eyes to grow hot with unshed tears.

'There, I think that's all.' He stood and moved to the sink, calling to her warningly as she moved. 'Stay there!' He seemed to have eyes in the back of his head.

'I'll leave this here,' he remarked, placing the dustpan with its dangerous contents on the top of the draining board. 'No doubt Sophia has some special way to get rid of glass.' He half turned. 'What are you doing down here anyway—getting a drink?'

'Yes.' Her dry lips made speaking difficult and she had to make two attempts at the answer, grateful that he had turned back to the sink to rinse his hands.

'Well, have you had one or not?' He looked at her impatiently and she had never felt so childish in her life. Caught by the headmaster stealing tuck. She felt her colour rising and moved to get down.

'Can't you ever do as you're told for even one second?' Andreas strode swiftly to her and stopped her stealthy slide to the ground. 'Do you want another drink, or was that enough?'

'I—I don't want one, thank you. I—I'll get back to bed now.'

'Yes,' he said grimly, staring furiously at her, 'get back to your neat little bed, Olivia. It should be sufficiently cold enough now even for you.'

Her unhappy sound of protest did not soften the expression on his face and he swung her up into his arms with no more difficulty that if she had been Nicky, striding to the door and depositing her in the hall.

'There, I imagine you can find your way up the stairs without any further danger?' He didn't say good night. He simply turned and marched off to the study, and she heard the door bang shut as she reached the bottom step of the stairs.

Pain clutched at her as fiercely as if the broken glass had penetrated her heart, and she stopped, her hand clutching her stomach, her head bent beneath the pain of her longing for man who did not love her.

'What's the matter?' He was coming silently across the hall, once again startling her into near panic, and she turned swiftly to the stairs.

'I—I thought you were in the study.'

'Only closing the door for the night.' He reached her side before she had even made the second step. 'I asked you what's the matter. I don't think you answered.'

'Nothing.' Olivia had to make herself look at him,

struggling to appear indifferent, but the sight of his face and his tightly angry mouth were too much and she turned away again, biting her lips to stifle the cry of pain that threatned to choke her.

'Olivia.' He spoke her name softly, but there was no gentleness in the hands that grasped her shoulders. 'What are you suffering from, *karithis mou*?' He turned her to him, tipping her unwilling face to the light, seeing the beginning of tears on her cheeks. 'Are you crying for Nicky or for me? What do you need, Olivia? This?'

He pulled her roughly into his arms, his deep searching kiss taking her breath away, his hands hard and uncompromising on her back. When he drew back to look into her eyes at the mute appeal in their green depths, his lips claimed hers again, burning the velvet softness of her mouth, his hands moving over her this time with savage sensuality until she arched against him, trembling and completely submissive.

'So, now we know what keeps you awake at night, my sleek little kitten, what brings you barefooted to the kitchen at midnight. You have a fiancé in the house, but I'm the one you need.' He swung her into his arms again, pushing her head to his shoulder and climbing the stairs steadily, his breathing uneven and fast, and she knew it was not this minor exertion that unsteadied him. There was a ferocious need in Andreas too, it showed in the heat of his body beneath the thin silk of the white shirt, in the tight grip of his hands.

He kicked the door closed as he carried her into his room and slid her to the floor beside the bed.

'If you wish to change your mind, my darling, now is the time to do it,' he rasped harshly. 'From this point on you will get no choice—and I warn you that I am not in a gentle mood. I want you as a starving man needs food, and such a man does not eat delicately.'

Olivia didn't answer, couldn't answer, and he pulled

her to him with savage intensity, his lips seeking hers with brutal force, cruelly crushing her mouth.

His urgency frightened her, but not as much as the desire that swept through her like a fire. She had always wanted him, but never with this sinking, burning intensity. She clung to him, her mind spinning and her body falling, only his iron grasp keeping her upright.

'Beautiful, so beautiful.' He slid her robe to the floor and pushed her delicate nightdress aside until it too fell like a softly drifting feather to the ground. 'But then I discovered that you were still beautiful last night, didn't I? Last night when we had our other assignation at midnight. You were so vulnerable then, Olivia, but perhaps not as vulnerable as you are now.'

His hands ran over her in long seductive caresses, his eyes following their progress.

'What do you expect of me, Olivia?' he murmured. 'What do you expect of a discarded husband who is about to lose you yet again? You expect tenderness? Generosity? I warn you that you will get neither, and it is too late now to back out of this. I could not let you go.'

The feverish glitter of his eyes told her that he was speaking only the truth, he was aroused as she had never seen him before, but she was lost completely as his hands closed over the fullness of her breasts.

'Olivia!' he groaned, and her mind began to reel again in a blind rapture that no threats of cruelty could disperse.

Andreas laid her on the bed, his eyes on her trembling limbs as he threw off his clothes with a wild abandon. For a second he stood before her, his eyes glazed over with passion, his face tight and hard.

'Remember me, Olivia?' He ground out harshly. 'Remember your husband who treated you with adoration and respect? You will remember me before this night is over, I promise you!'

He joined her on the bed, drawing her urgently into

his arms, but she held back, fear striking her at last.

'Please, Andreas!' It was a tight little whisper and he drew back his head impatiently, staring into her eyes like a stranger.

'Your body was saying that to me downstairs, my darling,' he breathed thickly, 'and it was not a plea for mercy. If you had wanted mercy you should have gone to your own bed and not come with me to mine.'

He pulled her to the hard length of his body, and a shock raced through her at the contact of her flesh with his, a shock she knew that he felt too, because he moaned aloud and sought her mouth with fevered urgency, his hands moving over her with savage desire, urging her yet closer, heating her skin and melting her until all fear left her and she arched against him, filled with the same frenzy that had him in its grip.

It was too late to escape, too late to think as she was swept into another world, her love for him softening her lips and melting her limbs until she was soft and responsive, her arms tightly around his neck.

Her warmth and surrender softened him too for a moment and his hands began to caress her gently, his searching mouth sweetening against hers, but the need between them allowed for no tenderness and her gripping arms and pleading body soon drove him into savagery, his ravaging hands and lips burning her face and throat, her slender shoulders, until she knew she would bear the marks for days.

'I can't be gentle, Olivia,' he groaned against her parted lips as he moved over her. 'I've waited too long, lost you for an eternity.' His hands pinched her skin and she knew that he too would carry the scars tomorrow as her nails scored his back.

She was helpless beneath him as he possessed her, her heart throbbing wildly against his, her mind soaring out of her control as his lips forced hers further apart and his steely hands held her fast.

She was sobbing quietly as she drifted down from the clouds, but Andreas didn't seem to hear her. His feelings were still unmanageable, she could tell that from the harshness of his breathing and the tight grip that he had on her battered body.

The tears wouldn't stop, and after a while he moved aside, looking down at her hot, tear-stained face in the soft lamplight.

'Come here.' His voice was roughened and the hands that held her were strong, but trembling slightly. He snuggled her against him, allowing her tears to flow unrestrainedly until eventually her body relaxed and her sobs became soft whimpers of unhappiness. He had taken her with a savage need, but she had known before that he wanted her and her need had been as great. Hers, though, was for love, and she had given herself to him with a greater love than she had ever felt, but he did not love her. That he could not, had never been able to resist her was no comfort, and she lay silently in the cradling arms, her misery, if anything, greater than before, because now she had no refuge, no self-respect. She had surrendered completely.

Andreas drew back after a while and looked at her again, his eyes unreadable, none of the triumph there that she would have expected to see.

'Tomorrow you will be bruised,' he said ruefully, his eyes moving over her skin. 'I have never bruised you before—but then we have never felt this need before, never been apart for three years before.' He looked at her intently. 'There has been no one else, has there, Olivia?' She shook her head and the tears threatened again, but he kissed her eyes with a return to his old tenderness. 'I knew that. You have never been anything but mine. If anyone else ever touched you, I would kill them.'

He reached for her hand and slowly drew the diamond ring from her finger, his eyes holding hers.

'You will not wear this again, Olivia,' he ordered. 'I have you back, and I do not intend to misplace you again ever.'

She didn't argue. She was back and she would stay, deep down she had known that ever since she had seen him again. His eyes gleamed at the unspoken submission in her face and his lips sought hers again, his hands stroking her until the fire spread through them both again with the same frightening ferocity.

Olivia woke up early. It was so long since she had slept in Andreas' arms that the unaccustomed weight of his hand on her breast, his arm across her flat stomach, woke her in the early hours. It was just daylight and the room was bathed in the peculiar cold grey light of a dawn that came up over the sea.

He was asleep, relaxed and peaceful, every line erased from his face, and for a few minutes she looked at him sadly, her love, her whole life. He would never know what that surrender had cost her, would cost her for the rest of her life, but she had some part of him and she had his son; she would stay.

She slid from the warmth of the bed, quietly gathering her clothes and creeping out into the passage and into her own room. The bruises were indeed there, she admitted as she looked at herself in the bathroom mirror. They were darker and more noticeable than she had thought, and she wondered how she was going to keep them covered.

She had a long hot shower and washed her hair, drying it and brushing it until it shone. She made up her face too, trying her best to erase the dark shadows from beneath her eyes that showed how little sleep she had had. Even so, her skills were not up to the task, and she had to admit that anyone with normal vision would be able to read her like a book, would know just where she had spent the night.

She was too tired and wretched to care; at least Nicky wouldn't know. Youth was a wonderful thing.

She dressed carefully as she waited for Nicky to wake up, and found a long-sleeved blouse that hid her arms, but nothing could hide her neck and the swollen evidence of her mouth. The collar that she turned up just about did it, so long as it stayed in place.

Nicky gave his morning shout and she went in to him at once. She couldn't face Andreas just yet, she needed at least another hour.

He still had not appeared when she had washed and fed Nicky and handed him over to an eager Tomas who wanted to walk him by the sea. Andreas was sleeping the sound sleep of the contented—after all, he had won—and Olivia stood looking out at the garden as Tomas hefted Nicky into his arms and went carefully down the long flight of steps to the beach.

A maid came in with her breakfast, and to her surprise, Peter appeared too, his face filled with a smugness that she would soon have to wipe from it. She didn't know where to begin and turned away, but he came forward quickly and stood in front of her, his back to the sea, the light full on her face.

'You look tired, Olivia. Are you all right?' She had no time to reply before his eyes widened and his hand shot out, moving her collar aside.

'My God!' He looked at her with complete disgust and her cheeks flamed under his stony stare. 'I don't need to ask why you're tired, do I? Now I know why you came back here. If that's the sort of thing you need, you're not likely to get it anywhere else, certainly not from me!'

He stood looking at her as he would have looked at a particularly disgusting client, and Olivia felt unable to defend herself. She felt that she owed him something for the kindness he had shown her in the past, for his willingness to be engaged to a woman who had been married before. It never occurred to her that she had rights at that moment, she could only feel guilt that she had let him down by not being the person he had thought her, by letting her love for Andreas override everything that Peter expected of her.

Clearly he thought that she was not a respectable girl, not a fit person to be even spoken to civilly, but in her guilt and embarrassment she was prepared to take everything he said, realising even as she stood with bowed head that if Andreas had loved her, she would never have stood for this.

'I should have realised that once back here you would revert to type. How old were you when you married him, Olivia? Eighteen? What happened? Couldn't you keep away from him? I expect that it was a relief to the old man when Skouradis finally married you. You cheap little . . .'

He was slammed back against the rail of the patio by one powerful brown hand as a strong arm gathered Olivia close.

'Say one more word to her, and I'll kill you here and now!' She didn't have to look round. Even if she had dared, it wasn't necessary. The savagery in the quiet voice said it all, stilling Peter's wicked tongue and increasing Olivia's trembling.

All the energy seemed to have left her body. She wanted to sink to the ground and hide her face, but Andreas held her upright, his arm never moving from her as he reached into his pocket.

'My wife came to return this to you.' His hand shot out and held the diamond ring under Peter's nose. 'You will eat your breakfast and then leave Illyaros. Now that I have Olivia back I would have perhaps been prepared to be generous with you, but no one speaks to Olivia in anything but respectful tones. Therefore—you will leave.'

There was deep colour in Peter's face as he struggled

between anger and fear. He had humiliated Olivia, but his own humiliation was uppermost in his mind as he glared at his host.

'Respectful!' he began scornfully, but one long finger was waved in front of his face.

'One word!' Andreas threatened. 'You will now pack.'

Without another word, Peter left the patio and Andreas released Olivia, turning on the startled maid who appeared in the doorway.

'Take Mr Challoner some breakfast in his room,' he ordered. 'He is in a hurry to leave us. Where is Tomas?' he enquired angrily, turning on Olivia, who had sunk to the nearest chair now that she was without his supporting arm.

'On the beach with Nicky.' She couldn't meet his eyes, and with a growl of annoyance that might have been directed at her, he strode into the garden and over to the edge of the steps, bellowing at the top of his voice for Tomas.

'Eat your breakfast,' he ordered tersely, striding back on to the patio, his anger nowhere near under control.

'I—I'm not hungry,' she began in a low voice, but he bellowed at her too, careless of anyone who might hear.

'Eat! My son's mother does not starve herself into ill health, neither does she shiver in shame that she has spent the night in her husband's arms.' His darkened face and furious eyes frightened her into picking up her fork and he turned away impatiently. She got the message; he was livid with her too.

Tomas appeared with astonishing rapidity, breathless from his dash up the long flight of steps, and Andreas held out his arms for Nicky, handing the startled child over almost at once to Sophia who had come to see what all the uproar was about.

'Entertain him for a while, Tia Sophia,' he said, softening his voice a little in deference to her age. She glanced quickly at Olivia, her face anxious, but Olivia managed a weak smile and shook her head. Intervention on her behalf by anyone at this moment would only bring violence on all their heads. Andreas was at his very worst. Sophia went off reasonably happy, she had Nicky to herself for a while.

'I want you to take Mr Challoner to Athens, Tomas,' Andreas said shortly, his face like granite.

'Boat or bird?' asked Tomas laconically, referring to the helicopter.

'Bird,' snapped Andreas. 'I would not wish his company too long on my best friend.'

There was a visible preening about Tomas at this remark, but he carefully avoided Olivia's eyes as he asked, 'He goes alone?'

'Alone—and now!' Andreas emphasised savagely as Peter appeared. He had clearly decided to do without breakfast in order to leave this house of iniquity as quickly as possible, and Tomas could hardly contain his delight as he moved to take the suitcase. The threat to the happiness of the whole house was going away and Tomas was proud to be able to be the instrument that removed it. He clearly thought that with this intruder gone and a beautiful child to care for, Olivia would remain for ever and things would return to normal, to a time when for him at least, the sun appeared to be always shining.

'Tomas will fly you to Athens,' Andreas told his unwelcome guest, his eyes hard as stones, but Peter was anything but happy at this arrangement. To him Tomas was nothing but a 'minder', a 'gorilla', as he had informed Olivia, and he surveyed the tightly packed muscles of the faithful Tomas with great misgiving.

'Can he fly?'

'Providing that he has a helicopter or a plane, yes,' Andreas assured him sarcastically. 'Do not worry, he can do everything that you are capable of doing and more besides. He is not a solicitor, but then who would wish to be?'

Tomas left, carrying the case, his grin now open and frank. He was taking the man who had threatened to steal Olivia and he could wish for nothing better.

Peter turned to follow him, his eyes deliberately turned from Olivia. She was cut completely from his mind and she could imagine his internal shudders as he considered how close he had come to making a terrible mistake. She knew him well enough to know that on his return flight he would be congratulating himself on an escape from near disaster, but she still felt deep guilt at her conduct towards him.

'Peter——' She moved to get up, but the word had hardly left her lips before she was slammed back into her chair by Andreas, his face thunderous.

'You will not speak to someone who has insulted you,' he ground out, 'not unless you wish to see him knocked down before your eyes. Of course I am prepared to do that, but I imagined that you would have liked to leave him some small amount of dignity.'

She was silent and he looked at her with grim satisfaction. It was easy to read his thoughts. She was back in her place, subdued and dutiful, the mother of his son.

'Goodbye, Mr Challoner,' he said pointedly as Peter still stood there, having paused as Olivia said his name. 'You will need a new secretary, and I suggest that the next time you plan to marry, you choose a widow or at least someone with less fire than Olivia. I feel that you would have been outclassed, whatever your plans were for the future.'

They were alone almost at once and Andreas did not speak, even when the sleek silver and red bird flew over the house on its way to Athens. He seemed to be attacking his breakfast with the same aggressive energy that had sustained him until now, and Olivia dared not either look at him, or speak.

Their frantic lovemaking of the night before had receded into the background at the moment and she did not want to do or say anything that would remind him of it; she certainly did not want to draw his eyes to her pale tired face, nor to the bruises that had precipitated this morning's events.

'The telephone, Kyrie Skouradis,' a very timid maid stuck her head round the door, adding when Andreas only glared, 'It is Despinis Kastakis from Athens.'

There was a moment's silence, a silence during which Olivia felt the very tenuous hold she had on the day slipping away. What she had expected after last night she didn't know, but she supposed that deep down she had thought that it must mean something more to Andreas than a night of passion.

A knife seemed to twist inside her as he prepared to rise, tossing down his napkin and finishing his coffee in one swift movement.

'Good, I am coming.' He rose and then glanced at the table. 'Bring more tea for my wife,' he ordered sternly as the maid disappeared, well aware that Kyne Skouradis was in one of his rages.

'I'm not your wife!' Olivia's hiss of anger stopped him in his tracks and he came back, jerking her face up as she sat white and shaken where he had left her.

'Then you are my mistress!' he snapped, his eyes boring into hers. 'After last night you can hardly call yourself an uninterested spectator, can you? Wife or mistress, it is all one to me. I have you back and you will stay.'

A few minutes later, ignoring the fresh tea that had been brought with alacrity, Olivia, passing through the hall, heard him on the phone.

'No, not today, Leandi. I have plenty to do and some things cannot be left. Tomorrow I would very much like to see you, but I'll telephone you later as to the time.'

She didn't stay to hear more. There was now a rage within her own heart that would help to sustain her. So he wanted two mistresses now, did he? She would show him how one of them could behave, she would show him too how the mother of his son could behave.

She stormed into the kitchen and collected Nicky from Sophia, offering no explanation, too angry to speak even to her. In her heart at this moment they were all guilty, all in league with Andreas to turn her life into a misery. If they thought that she would not fight back, then they were mistaken.

Andreas was back on the patio as she marched through it on her way to the garden, and the smile that came into his eyes at the sight of his son died slowly as he saw Olivia's grim face.

'Where are you going?' he asked as she brushed past him, giving him no time to have his first words of the day with Nicky.

'Down to the beach.' She did not pause, nor turn as he spoke again.

'I'll come with you.' He made a move towards her and she faced him, her scathing eyes and her angry expression stopping him.

'We prefer to be alone, thank you,' she said coldly. 'We are more used to being alone than being in company.' At that moment Nicky wound his arms around her neck and crooned in his soft way, no glance at the man who had so recently come into his life, and his little action helped her. It also stopped Andreas in his tracks.

My weapon, Olivia thought bitterly, remembering the look Andreas had had on his face when he had hesitated to intrude on the bathtime play. She would make him feel an intruder, she had more than a two years' advantage. She could make Andreas suffer very easily. Power, rage and money would not buy love. Nicky was hers and would stay hers.

She glanced triumphantly at Andreas, a tight smile on her lips when she saw that he very clearly understood. He made no further move to join them as she made her way to the steps.

Her rage sustained her throughout the day. She played with Nicky on the beach until he was tired, ignoring the fact that twice when she looked up Andreas was watching from the wall that surrounded the garden. If there was a forlorn air about him then it was so much the better; unhappiness was something that he would have to get used to.

He was nowhere in sight as she gave Nicky his lunch and put him down for his afternoon nap, staying in her room until he woke up. At dinner too she managed to cut Andreas out completely by heaving the heavy highchair up the stairs to her grandfather's room and feeding Nicky there. The excuse, if she had needed one, was that he had seen little of his great-grandson, but she realised as she was doing it that she needed no excuse.

Andreas held her because she had Nicky and because she loved them both, but he could not demand either her love or her co-operation. Neither could he order his son to love him. He was vulnerable in this regard, as she had been when he had taken her to his bed, and the thought gave her a grim satisfaction.

He had seen her heaving the chair upstairs when she had attained almost the top step and his sudden halting in the hall, his narrow-eyed glance of understanding, had pleased her immensely. If he chose to come into her grandfather's room and join them, then he came as an intruder. He did not come.

At bathtime, she locked the door, and when Nicky was settled for the night, she had her meal served with the old man, taking a delight in talking about her son, telling Alex Skouradis little anecdotes, little incidents

that made Nicky's short past seem real and close.
Making up to Alex for all the time he had missed.
Giving him information that Andreas did not have, her
bitter heart and mind wilfully glad to rob Andreas of
these small things.

She sank into bed that night with a smile of
determined satisfaction. The few times she had seen
Andreas had shown her that he had taken this badly,
not with anger, but with a great deal of pain. She settled
her pillows comfortably. There were many ways of
being trapped and in trapping her, Andreas had
inadvertently trapped himself. He would never really
have Nicky without her ready co-operation, and he
would never get that.

CHAPTER NINE

OLIVIA awoke in the night to the sound of thunder; the threatened storm had arrived. For a while she lay peacefully, glad that her curtains were opened to the brilliant night, to the sharp jagged streaks of lightning that tore through the black sky.

Many times as a child she had lain here and watched the scene that she was watching now, the fabulous display of lightning across the heavens, the forked light hitting the hills in the distance, the crashing thunder rolling across an angry sea and crashing around the old house with menace and splendour.

She had never been afraid of these storms that sometimes came rapidly and violently in this part of the world. Her wild romantic nature had always enjoyed the majestic displays, the brilliant light and the awesome sound. She had welcomed the storm as she welcomed it now.

It took her a few minutes to realise that she was not alone to enjoy it now. There was Nicky, and he had never met anything of this magnitude in his life.

With a gasp of self-disgust, she leapt from the bed, grabbing her robe and tying it hastily as she ran from the room. He would be terrified!

His door was partly open, the soft nightlight still burning as she hurried into the room—only to stop in bewilderment at the sight of Andreas standing beside the little white bed. He did not look round and she stood quite still, her eyes on his sombre figure.

He had evidently been in bed and had had the same thoughts. His black hair was still untidy from sleep, his lean brown body covered in a dark bathrobe that stopped at his bare legs.

'I—I thought the storm would have wakened him.' It was a very obvious remark, but what else could she say? He had thought about Nicky long before she had.

'Yes, I thought the same thing, but he appears to be impervious to the noise, or perhaps like you he enjoys the sound of a raging storm.'

His eyes were still on the sleeping child, and Olivia saw his misery with a lurching of her heart that she could not prevent. There was love on his face and a hopelessness that she had never thought to see on that strong, determined countenance. She had won her game with so little effort that she was stunned by the size of her victory. Andreas knew that she could keep his son from him even though he held them both prisoners, and his defeated look told her just how clearly he knew.

Suddenly she wanted no victory. She never wanted to see that proud head bowed as it was now. Rather than that, she would suffer herself. She loved Andreas too much to see him suffer.

She turned away, prepared to leave him a clear field, prepared to hand him her victory on a plate.

'I—I'll go back to bed. I don't think he needs two of us, and as you're here . . .'

'Olivia!' The tormented voice stopped her in her tracks, but she did not turn, it would not do to let him see what was on her face now. 'Don't go, Olivia,' he begged. 'He may not need you, but I do. He's lucky, he can sleep, dream and wake up to the certainty of your arms. I have no such good fortune.'

She stood stock still, unable to believe her ears, terrified that she was imagining this in her unhappiness, but his voice went on, soft and dark, his misery so evident that she had to believe it.

'I thought after last night . . . I thought that there must be something there, that even after your determination to leave me, to marry someone else, there must be some feeling left. Was it just a physical need, Olivia? Has all that we've been to each other come down at last to that?'

What was he saying? Did he want her to tell him that she loved him more than ever? Was this the final price she had to pay? She could find no words to answer and stood with bowed head by the door, knowing that he would soon tire of trying to plead with her. It was not in his proud nature to plead with anyone, man or woman.

'Today you've cut me from your life. You don't need to go away to leave me, do you? Oh, you're clever, my little witch, I've always known that. I know what hell you've prepared for me and I know that I'll be forced to live in it.'

'I'll not keep Nicky from you.' She turned then, her eyes glazed with tears. 'I won't do that again. I was angry, but I know you want him, I know you need him as much as I do.'

'Thank you.' Her offer had not eased the look of suffering on his face. 'I know that to say that you've surrendered the weapon you were going to defeat me with, but I give it back to you, to hold in your hand for ever if you wish.'

'Then what . . .?' She stared at his sombre face, unable to understand, and he just looked at her, his dark eyes on hers.

'It's not what I want, Olivia.' He took a half step towards her and then stopped, unsure of himself for the first time in his life as far as she knew. 'I want you, Olivia. I want you, not like last night. I want you body and soul. Nothing else will ever do for me.'

Olivia didn't know what he meant, didn't know what his words really meant. He was not confessing love for her, he was just pleading a deep need, a need to own her as he had once done, but she could no more bear to see his suffering now than she could have gone on making him suffer with Nicky, and there was nothing but love in her heart and on her face as she ran into the arms that lifted instantly to hold her.

'Olivia. Sweet, sweet Olivia!' He rocked her against him, his arms claiming her tightly and she wound her own slim arms around his neck, covering his tanned face with frantic kisses, feeling her bitterness ebb away as she poured again the love that she had never lost on to this tall proud man who held her.

'Andreas! Oh, Andreas. Don't you know that you have me already, body and soul?'

He tightened his arms and swung her up against his hard chest, his kisses gentle on her face.

'Then let us leave this young man to sleep through the storm, because without you beside me I think I'll never be able to sleep again.'

The bed was soft and cool against her skin as moments later she lay beside him, his hands stroking her tenderly as he looked into the green depths of her eyes. His fingers trailed over her skin and he frowned as he saw the bruises that he had inflicted the night before.

'Last night I behaved like a heathen,' he murmured regretfully. 'But tonight I will love you as I've never loved you before. I won't hurt you, my little Olivia.'

'I behaved like a heathen too,' she whispered, her fingers finding the scratches she had made on his smooth brown shoulders. But he smiled wickedly.

'That I did not mind in the least. You were always afraid to respond to me before. It was your fire that drove me to such savagery last night.' He cupped her swollen breast in strong brown fingers. 'But tonight, little kitten, I will call the tune, I will set the pace. It is a long time until morning when the monster will awake and demand that I give you up.'

His lovemaking was slow and gentle, generous and tender, filling her with happiness, wiping away the misery of the years she had been without him. He kissed every part of her, lingering as if he could never have enough of her, arousing her as his tempestuous passion of the night before had never aroused her, slowing her down and pacing her to his demands when she cried out in frustration.

'Slowly, my little sweet, we have a whole night for this and I want to enjoy every minute of you. I want you to enjoy every minute of me.'

His skilful lips and hands controlled her, owned her, until he was finally ready to give her what she cried out for, possessing her with a groan of pleasure that drowned her own cry of delight.

He was smiling into her eyes as she finally drifted back to earth, not crying this time as she had done the night before, but turning at once to nestle in his arms.

'Not so fast, my kitten,' he laughed. 'Just because you are sleek and contented it does not mean that I have finished with you yet.' He laughed aloud at her expression of shock and shook his head. 'I want to talk to you, that's all—at the moment.'

He moved his dark head on the pillow so that he could see her face clearly.

'Tell me, my darling, are you happy, are you happy now?'

For a moment she hesitated. Yes, she had been until he said that. Now she could see Leandi Kastakis, her dark head on some pillow beside Andreas.

'You had better tell me, I think.' His dark eyes were now still and shuttered. 'You are not, I hope, regretting that Challoner has gone?'

'No!' Her reaction was sufficiently strong to satisfy him and his smile appeared again.

'Then what?'

It never occurred to him that she was not content to share him with another woman, any more than he would have been content to share her with another man. The realisation stilled her tongue and drained away some of the contentment on her face. She did not want to spoil this time, but he persisted, holding her unwilling face to the lamplight and ordering her to tell him.

'Leandi——' she began, but he stopped her by covering her opened lips with his, pulling her tightly into his arms and devouring her for long minutes until she lay back breathless and trembling.

'Tomorrow, Olivia mine,' he promised softly. 'Tomorrow we will discuss Leandi. Tonight is too short for such a big subject, but I promise you that tomorrow we will have a day of reckoning, in more ways than one.'

She had to be content with that, and soon Leandi was again forgotten as his eager arms closed around her, his heated kisses reawakened her to passion.

Andreas was dressed when she awoke the next morning, and his eyes were the first thing she saw as he crouched beside the bed, trailing his fingers over her skin, his lips softened in a teasing smile.

'At last—I have been trying to wake you up for ages.' He stood, lean and handsome in black shirt and black jeans, his hair neatly brushed and shining. He looked fresh and alive, and Olivia sank beneath the sheets as he looked at her. She felt wildly untidy and tried to hide herself.

'Nicky——' she began, glancing at the clock and finding that it was already seven-thirty.

'All under control,' he reported, pushing her back when she made to get up. 'We have him downstairs, washed and dressed and almost fed. Tomas is hanging around with the clear intention of fighting Sophia if she does not hand Nicky over to him. If you remember, he was frustrated in his desire to get Nicky to himself yesterday.'

'Yes, I remember,' she countered. 'You were yelling at the top of your voice, unless my memory fails me.'

'Yes, I was, wasn't I?' he agreed, looking not the least bit repentant. He suddenly sat on the bed and lifted her into his arms. 'I want you to stay in bed this morning and have a rest. I've told everyone that you are not to be disturbed. In a few minutes, Sophia will send you some nice toast and tea and a little boiled egg,' he teased, 'and then you can lie here and sleep or rest until lunchtime.'

'I'll feel too guilty and lazy,' she complained, but he was adamant.

'Today you can be lazy until lunchtime. You need to rest, I have not been too happy that you are so thin and pale. Now we will get you back to normal.'

'Yes, master,' she grinned, looking up into his dark determined eyes. 'And if Nicky also wishes to make demands?'

'He'll have to get past me first,' Andreas promised, 'and as I told you before, he is too small to win at the moment.'

He stood up after putting her back gently on the pillow.

'I'll see that you are awakened in good time to have lunch with me.' She moved to get out of bed, but he towered over her threateningly. 'And you stay in this bed, Olivia—my bed!'

His smile broke again as she nodded, blushing and confused.

'I especially want you to have lunch with me today, Olivia,' he said softly. 'Until then I'll leave you to rest. I have a lot to do.'

After her promised breakfast had been cleared away, Olivia lay back and allowed her mind to think about her situation. How did things stand now? Last night and still this morning, there had been no anger in Andreas. Everything about him, his words, his looks, his behaviour, had been as they used to be. She could have almost believed that he loved her if it had not been for Leandi Kastakis, but the Greek girl was still very much in the picture.

It was useless to try to sleep for even though her body felt languorous and content, her mind would not give up the worrying about the day that faced her. Today, he had said they would talk about Leandi and he had meant it, but what would he say? Was he about to offer her an arrangement whereby he still kept the best of both worlds? The thought was unbearable.

In spite of her misgivings and inner fears, Olivia did sleep, awakening when Sophia knocked on the door an hour before lunch-time and brought in a fresh cup of tea.

'Andreas said you were to be wakened now, Olivia,' she said more quietly than was her normal way, and Olivia's face flushed when she realised that Sophia was avoiding her eyes.

She was lying drowsy and warm in this bed and she had never faced Sophia before in this situation. The stinging reproof she had received from Peter was still very much in the forefront of her mind, and her tentative smile died unhappily as Sophia turned abruptly away and made for the door.

'Is Nicky all right?' There was another source of guilt. She had never had any time to herself since he was born. Her free time, when she was not at work, had been taken up entirely with her son, and now she was lying here, neglecting him.

'Of course he is, Olivia.' Sophia turned and saw Olivia's anxious face. 'Don't worry, child, he is fine. You need some small time of your own. I know what your life must have been.'

'I know there's something wrong,' Olivia began. 'If it's because I'm in here, Aunt Sophia ...'

'Oh, Olivia, you foolish girl!' Sophia came back

towards the bed, exasperation and anxiety making a bewildering mixture on her face. 'Where else should you be but here? Do you think that I did not realise since your marriage that you slept in your husband's bed?' She paused and looked away uneasily. 'It's not that, Olivia, it's just that I had thought—had hoped—with Nicky's arrival and now seeing you here, knowing all morning that you were resting here because Andreas ordered it—we all hoped that things were at last as they should be. I can't understand anything any more. Perhaps I'm growing too old, perhaps I'm even older than Alex. The behaviour of Andreas is beyond me.' She looked uneasily at Olivia and turned away again. 'We will see, we will see. He was always so kind, so understanding. Now I just don't know any more.'

She was gone before Olivia could even begin to understand what she was talking about. Something was upsetting Sophia, something new, and her own uneasiness increased as she dressed to go down for lunch, taking the full hour that was left, showering and washing her hair and lingering as long as possible so that she would not have to face whatever new misery was waiting for her.

Sophia's unhappy face had told her all too clearly that she would have to be prepared for some sort of shock, something that had shocked Sophia. She felt that today, after last night, she could face nothing more, her defences were all destroyed.

Nevertheless, she had to go down and she did, stopping in surprise to find the sunlit patio empty. Lunch was usually served there, and when she was told by a passing maid that today the meal was to be served in the dining room, a chill of fear caught her in its grip. There had to be some reason for this formality and she had no idea what it could be.

She found out soon enough. It took some courage to open that dining-room door and walk inside, but her

courage fled at once as she faced the amused gaze of
Leandi Kastakis.

The Greek girl was sitting at the table already, her
dark skin and black hair giving an exotic background
to the white suit and bright red blouse that she wore.
For a second, Olivia stood looking at her, unable to
believe this. Andreas had brought his mistress into their
own home. She had never been here since the night of the
engagement as far as Olivia knew, and now, after last
night, after this morning's gentleness, he had prepared
this cruel encounter for her.

She understood now why Sophia had been so uneasy,
had declared that she could no longer understand
Andreas. With this blow he had shattered any dreams
that Olivia had cherished and there was nothing now
but to accept defeat and bow before this monstrous
indignity, or to go away and leave everything that made
life possible.

She turned with a soft cry of pain and searched
blindly for the door.

'Olivia!' Andreas' hands on her arms stopped her, but
she refused to look at him. 'Wait, Olivia. I promised
you a reckoning and the time is now.'

'You imagine that I'm going to calmly take lunch
with her? What do you think I am, Andreas? Let me
go!' She pulled away in a frenzy of pain and
humiliation, but he caught her again and forced her to
turn, his arms now completely round her as he stood
behind her so that they were facing the amused eyes of
Leandi Kastakis. The situation was no embarrassment
to her, she sat at ease, her dark eyebrows raised in
sardonic speculation, completely sure of herself—as
well she might be, thought Olivia unhappily.

'There is some talking to do, Leandi,' Andreas said
with a calm reason in his voice. 'Things cannot of
course be allowed to drift now that Olivia is home.' He
stressed the word, and for the first time, a flicker of

unease crossed Leandi's face. 'So tell her, Leandi, tell her just how long you have been my mistress. Tell Olivia about our love life. She is uneasy about it and I feel that she now should know the truth.'

Olivia struggled, desperate to escape from this torment, but he wound his arms around her waist more tightly still. The arms that she plucked at were like steel and the strength of his body behind her made escape impossible.

'Patience, Olivia,' he murmured against her hair, his dark eyes on Leandi. 'She will tell you all you need to know.'

'I think that this is too much, Andreas!' There was a sharp note of panic in the Greek girl's voice, a flush of colour under her skin. 'You can't mean it!'

'Oh, but I do,' he purred softly. 'Come now, Leandi, are you ashamed to own me as a lover? Tell Olivia all about our affair.'

Leandi sprang to her feet and Olivia felt the increased tension in Andreas when it appeared that Leandi meant to walk out of the room.

'Tell her!' His voice was louder now, threatening. 'Tell her the truth, because if you do not, then I promise you that I will take reprisals against your family in such a way that you will never again have the wealth that seems to be your sole reason for existence. I will crush your father's business and put you all on the streets. You will find that Alex Skouradis is a child beside me when it comes to pitiless punishments!'

Leandi stood for a moment staring at him as if she had seen him clearly for the first time. She was pale now, and Olivia found herself fascinated by the tremor of Leandi's lips, her shaking hands.

'Well?' His voice was a low growl that contained not one shred of pity, his arms still tight and imprisoning around Olivia.

'I ... we—we have never been ... lovers.' It was

wrung from Leandi in a tortured voice as she was
forced to face Olivia. 'We were once friends, but never
more than that. It's true!' She looked with hatred at
Olivia and scornfully lifted her chin. 'You poor fool! If
it had been I, there would have been no divorce, no
flight away from Andreas. I would have fought.'

'Yes, you would,' Andreas said softly. 'You would
have fought to keep your hands on my wealth, to keep
the name of a wealthy husband. Olivia, though, fled
and accepted nothing if she could not have all my love.
You saw to that, did you not, Leandi? I do not know
how you managed the little scene so well. I have
thought about it for three years of sleepless nights.'

'I got a phone call,' Olivia whispered, and heard
Andreas take a sharp breath.

'I too,' he said softly, 'just before you burst in on the
little scene that had been prepared for your eyes. When
I lifted the receiver, there was no answer, but two
seconds later Leandi fainted, would have fallen if I had
not caught her. It was a signal, was it not?' he grated,
his eyes filled with rage.

'Yes!' Leandi had nothing to lose now. 'Takis
phoned, to both of you, and you walked right into it,
didn't you?' Her eyes turned to Olivia, filled with scorn,
and then back to Andreas. 'She was too young, always
too young. If she had not come to Illyaros, you and I
would have been married long ago. But she appeared
on the scene, and you were more content to take care of
a thin ungainly child than to look around you.'

'Yes, I was,' he agreed, his lips brushing Olivia's hair,
the gentle caress only serving to infuriate Leandi
further. 'I suppose that I have seen no one else since she
came, pale and frightened, into my life.'

'You'll tire of her!' Leandi stood, shaking now with
fury, clenching and unclenching her hands, the long
nails wanting to scratch at Olivia, but fear of Andreas
kept her in check. 'She has nothing to give you.'

'She has given me everything,' Andreas corrected her quietly, and at that moment the door opened and Sophia came in, her natural reticence subdued in her determination to have happiness back in this house again, her instincts telling her that only Olivia could bring it. She was holding Nicky in her arms, a defiance on her face that brought a smile at last to the grim and angry face of Andreas.

'Most fortuitous,' he murmured. 'My son Nicky, Leandi, another miracle that Olivia has performed, and let me correct your statement. I would never have married you whether I had ever met Olivia or not. Such thoughts were in your own greedy mind, never in mine.' He signalled to Sophia and she left. She had heard enough to ease her mind, she had seen his arms around Olivia.

'I suppose that you came in your own launch,' he asked with deceptive quiet, and Leandi nodded, the fight now completely gone from her.

'Takis brought me.' This information did not please Andreas either.

'Then you can go,' he told her harshly. 'Understand also that you are never to set foot on this island again, in fact it would be advisable if you were to become invisible, because if I should ever see you again I will be reminded that because of you, Olivia and I have lost three years of our lives. We have a son to show for it, but he can never make up for the separation. I do not make idle threats, Leandi. Any further interference in our lives and I will crush the Kastakis business affairs into powder and leave you all penniless!'

He turned Olivia slowly to face him after Leandi's footsteps had died away.

'Now you understand?' His dark eyes were penetrating and she nodded, still unable to speak. She had been too young, too young to be suspicious, except of Andreas. She felt her lack of trust, her desertion, like a weight on her heart, amazed that he could even consider forgiving her when he was so proud, so strong. Even so, she remembered the fact that he had left her to her own fate for three years.

'Olivia,' he began, seeing the bewilderment on her face, knowing as he always did what was in her heart. 'I realised that this must be the explanation very soon after you ran away, but I was angry with you, uncertain. I wanted you to realise the truth for yourself. I wanted you to love me enough to be certain that I would never betray you.'

'How do you know I love you enough now?' She looked up at him, her green eyes wide and appealing, and he smiled wickedly, lifting her face up to his.

'Oh, my Olivia,' he laughed, 'you think I do not know? After last night?'

He kissed her passionately, his arms tightly around her, moving back with reluctance when the door opened and her grandfather appeared, walking with the aid of Tomas.

'Grandfather!' Olivia was shocked and worried, but Andreas retained his hold on her, pulling her against him, unwilling to share her even with Alex.

'Don't let him worry you, *eros mou*,' he said softly. 'He has been walking slowly for weeks, but your sympathy is easier to gain when he is sitting in a wheelchair and playing at being Methuselah.'

Olivia was startled to see her grandfather blush brightly as she turned scandalised eyes upon him.

'I wanted you to stay and sort things out with Andreas,' he muttered gruffly. 'Somebody had to make things right and it clearly had to be me.' He looked away as Andreas regarded him sardonically, his eyebrows raised.

'I want to talk to Olivia—alone,' he said stubbornly. 'It's time she knew a few things.'

'You don't have to Alex,' Andreas put in quickly, but the old man waved his hand impatiently.

'It's time, it's time,' he insisted harshly. 'Leave us for a while, Andreas, you'll get her back.'

For a moment she thought that Andreas was about to refuse to leave, but after one long hard look at the old man he nodded and signalling to Tomas left the room, closing the door quietly behind them.

'Sit down, Olivia.' Whatever Alex Skouradis had to say, he clearly meant to say it at once, and Olivia sat down abruptly on the nearest chair. All her anxieties were there again, bubbling to the top, making her head spin.

'I expect we had better begin at the beginning and make a clean breast of it,' he muttered, avoiding her eyes, and suddenly she knew what he was going to tell her.

'It's all right, Grandfather. I know that you made Andreas marry me. I've always known. Don't distress yourself about that.'

'Made him marry you?' He sat upright in his chair, his craggy face alight with surprise and disbelief as she told him about the quarrel she had heard the week before the engagement.

'I know you wanted the family business tied up and that you wanted an heir for everything,' she finished sadly.

'Olivia!' He looked at her in total frustration. 'I never thought that any daughter of mine would give birth to an idiot, but you seem to be proving me wrong time and time again. You pick your ideas right out of the blue with no basis in fact whatever. Girl—you know him— do you imagine that anyone could order him to do something that he did not want to do? Yes, we had a quarrel, and yes, it was about you, but it was not what you seem to have been thinking for over three years.'

He looked at her angrily and then her white face and trembling hands softened him and he reached for her hand, patting it gently.

'Andreas wanted to marry you, Olivia. I was the one who was against it. You were too young, and in that I have been proved right. You never had a chance to look around and see anyone or anything but Andreas,' he smiled grimly. 'Andreas saw to that. He was fiercely possessive about you, and I told him that I would not allow any marriage between you for some years. Of course as usual, he got the better of me.'

'How?' The happiness she felt at the news only added to her bewilderment.

'How? Oh, easily enough. He wanted you and made it quite clear that he would have you, with or without my consent, married or not.' He shrugged his shoulders. 'I'm not blind, I saw how you felt, the air between you was so full of it, it was like being in an electric storm—what could I do but agree?' He frowned at her, almost as fierce as Andreas when he was displeased.

'You imagine that I would use you to secure anything for the business? It was always for Andreas. I decided that as soon as I saw him. Business affairs are not for women, you know my thoughts on that.'

She did. Women were for wives and mothers, to be pampered or subdued according to the whim of their husbands.

'He left me in England,' she said quietly. 'He gave up easily.' It all came down to that now.

She was startled to see her grandfather's look of guilt, in fact for a second he turned his face away as if to hide from her, but he quickly turned back.

'That's why I'm here. You can blame me for that,' he advised quietly. 'Blame it on me and on the past.'

Olivia would have spoken, but he held up his hand and stopped her.

'I have to tell you,' he said sombrely. 'I hate to think that you will feel badly about me, think less of me, but it must be said. I owe it to Andreas and to you.'

Olivia was silenced, sitting quietly as he struggled to find the words to begin.

'After the war,' he began quietly, his mind clearly in the past, 'things were in a turmoil, many factions struggling to gain the upper hand, and I made the mistake that no good business man makes, I backed one of them. I put all my eggs in one basket—the wrong basket, as it turned out. The others never forgave me and I had a hard struggle to keep the business. I had to fight in any way that I could and I was little concerned with the feelings of others.' He shot her a nervous look. 'Let us say that in my climb back to fortune, I rode roughly over others and made many enemies.'

He paused, but Olivia did not speak. To tell her that he had worked on the edge of dishonesty was a blow to him, but he seemed determined to continue.

'I held off handing the business over to Andreas for as long as I could, but eventually he had to take over and eventually he had to find out. He became afraid for you. There was so much hatred for me personally that he was afraid they would transfer their attention to you in order to get at me. He thought you might be kidnapped, and as he had also become obsessed with the idea that he had forced you into marrying him, then he felt that it was better to leave you in safety in England.'

He sighed deeply and looked across at her.

'Things settled down, I should have know that. There was no point in carrying on many years of hatred when Andreas took over the business—in any case, they like him, he helps everyone who needs it, without favour or expected reward. I used to think he was too soft, but now I'm not too sure. He gets deals that would never have been offered to me. After I became ill, Andreas still refused to send for you, being, as I said, obsessed with the idea that he had forced you into marriage when you were too young. I had to take matters into my own hands before you grew too far apart.'

He looked up at her from beneath shaggy brows, his old eyes anxious.

'Did I do wrong, Olivia? Am I just an old fool?'

'Oh, Grandfather, you're a wonderful old fool!' Olivia ran forward to hug him to her. 'Forget the past. We'll all be happy now, I just know it.'

She expected to find Andreas in his study, but he wasn't there and she finally tracked him down in the master bedroom. He was staring disconsolately at the ceiling and sat up abruptly as she came in.

'Well?' He eyed her anxiously.

'Well, what?' She was dying to rush into his arms, to feel his kisses, but the moment was too sweet to rush.

'Damn it, Olivia, what did Alex say?'

'Just what you expected him to say, I imagine.' She went to the mirror and combed her hair with his comb until he got up in exasperation and grabbed her.

'Stop fiddling about!' He spun her to face him. 'How did you take it? Are you angry with him, disgusted?'

'Of course not! The past is the past. It's all over.'

Angrily he pulled her to him, tightening his arms around her and then lifting her and tossing her on to the great double bed.

'I don't want the past to be over!' He glared down at her. 'I want everything to be as it was. I want to go back three years and find everything the same.'

'They're not the same, Andreas,' Olivia said softly. 'They're so much better, darling.'

With a groan he came down beside her, sinking into the arms that reached for him and pillowing his head on her breast.

'Oh, Andreas, I love you so much. I've caused you so much unhappiness.'

'You?' He raised his head, his startled eyes on her

face. 'You are all I've ever wanted, all I've ever needed. You were always my joy.'

'I ran away.' Her anxiety and guilt brought a smile to his face and his hand reached out to tenderly stroke her hair.

'You ran away because you were too young to be sure of me. It was a risk that I took when I insisted upon marrying you then. I was terrified of losing you and terrified that one day you would grow up and look around and ask yourself why you had ever agreed to marry me. When I saw that you were engaged, I thought that my worst nightmares had come true.' He looked down at her ruefully. 'Had I been a gentleman, I would have calmly handed you over and wished you happiness, but I still wanted you for myself. I was in a rage and a panic from the moment that I saw that ring on your finger.'

'You weren't very nice before you saw the ring,' Olivia accused. 'You were horrid to me at the airport.'

'Was I?' he grinned to himself, and shot a quizzical look at her. 'I wanted to pick you up and love you the moment I saw you. How would you have liked that, my fiery little cat?'

'At the time, not much,' Olivia admitted. 'I thought I hated you.'

'Did you?' Andreas looked so forlorn that she wound her arms around his neck and clung to him.

'Only until I saw you again. I suppose I never stopped wanting you to come and fetch me. Then you treated me right away as if I was an idiot child.'

His teeth nibbled at her tender earlobe, his hands stroking her gently as he lifted his head and looked deeply into her eyes.

'I never knew how to treat you after I realised that I wanted you, that I was in love with you. I never expected it to happen, it hit me like a thunderbolt, long before it happened to you,' he added with a teasing look. 'One moment it seemed that you were my wild, sunbright little girl and the next, everything in my life had changed, I wanted you for ever. I knew I could never let you go to anyone else.' He sighed. 'How could I know how to treat you? I wanted you both, the woman and the girl. I could not let either of them go. I refused to let you grow in case you found someone else. Then I blamed you for not growing.'

He rolled on to his back and stared at the ceiling moodily.

'I only wish I had been with you when you needed me,' he said in soft anguish. 'That I could have seen you with Nicky when he was a small baby.'

'Oh, Andreas!' she cried softly. 'I'm sorry I robbed you of all that, of seeing Nicky when he was smaller.'

'It's not that, *eros mou*,' he assured her, turning his head to look at her with deep love. 'I would have wanted to see my little wife turn into the mother of my child. You are an accomplished mother now and I have missed all the joy of seeing it happen.'

'There'll be other children, Andreas,' she said urgently, raising herself above him to look into his face, anxious to spare him any more hurt. But his face darkened at once and he grasped her tightly, pulling her on top of him and holding her protectively.

'Never!' he said adamantly. 'You will never face that again, Olivia. Your Aunt Beth told me about your pain and suffering when I went to fetch Nicky. You will never face that again because of me.'

'But I want to! Don't you realise that you're treating me like a child again? I want to have your babies, Andreas.'

Instantly she was trapped beneath him as he turned, his eyes dark and sensuous.

'Don't talk like that, darling. I can't resist you as it is.'

His hands grew urgent on her skin, but she held him

away, intent on talking to him, desperate that there should never be any more doubts and misunderstandings between them.

'I want to,' she whispered softly. 'Don't be afraid for me, darling. This time it will be all right—and anyway,' she smiled into his adoring eyes, 'it was worth it. I thought Nicky would be all I ever had of you.'

His kisses told her just how wrong she had been, and when he finally let her go, settling her into the curve of his arm where he could look into her winsome face, he smiled teasingly.

'Did you really mean to marry Challoner?'

She was at once alarmed, filled with dread, her face losing its colour.

'It ... I would have done—I ... think I would. Everything seemed to be over. You never came and commanded me to come back. Andreas! What if I had?' The panic in her eyes had him holding her tight.

'Hush, *karithia mou*, hush. You see how foolish I am. Even now I don't know how to treat you, even now I am jealous of an impossibility.'

'But what if ...'

'I would have come for you,' he said firmly, his eyes stern and unyielding. 'You are mine. I would have taken you away. Let us not ever speak of him again.'

'About the new baby,' she said quietly after he had loved her back to security. 'It may be too late already.' She smiled mischievously. 'It didn't take us long to produce Nicky. I think we're well suited, don't you?'

'Very compatible,' laughed Andreas after one anxious look at her. 'I suppose you thought of this last night?'

'It did cross my mind,' she admitted, smiling up at him.

He looked at her thoughtfully for one moment and then nodded.

'All right. In two weeks, I am taking you on a second honeymoon. Nicky can stay here and be spoiled,' he added as she opened her mouth to protest. 'I want you to myself.'

Olivia liked that and said so fervently without words, and later he added,

'We'll go to Bermuda. I've never had the chance to take you there. On the way back we'll call in London and see a few specialists. They can tell us if it will be all right—this time—and if they have any doubts, I'll have a team here for the event even if they have to be bought outright. Your Aunt Beth can come and stay here too if she will. She can help you and keep your grandfather out of our hair. Alex has a love-hate relationship with that lady, I think.'

Olivia was overjoyed, but her face fell a second later and he asked anxiously what was wrong, not wanting to see her sad ever again.

'I can't go on a second honeymoon, Andreas,' she whispered, blushing hotly. 'I'm not married to you any more.'

His shout of laughter was a joy and he clutched her tightly to him.

'Oh, Olivia, my own love! You cannot go on honeymoon because we are not married, and yet not two minutes ago you were pleading with me to give you another baby!' His eyes were teasing as he looked into her flushed face. 'Do you love me that much?' he asked softly.

'More,' she promised. 'More than anything in the world.'

'And I love you, my own darling,' he whispered, 'so much so that I am prepared to marry you again. The whole village, including the priest, will think I am mad, but if it will make you happy, then I am willing to be thought insane.'

He sat up and reached into a drawer in the bedside cabinet, turning with dark loving eyes to hold out his hand and show her the rings that he had kept there.

'I've held these in my hand every night since you went away. Will you wear them again, my darling?'

Tears started to her eyes as she saw the glittering emerald, the beautifully embossed golden band that had joined her to Andreas.

He slipped the emerald on to her finger and when she looked at him, startled to see that he intended to return the wedding ring to its box in the drawer, he smiled gently.

'Here,' he said softly, 'you are my wife still. When Mother Church has joined us there can be no separation, but I know that little English part of your mind that will not be still, and so I think we will save this until we marry again, but it had better be soon.'

There was a soft tap on the door—Sophia.

'I've put Nicky down for his nap,' she called. 'And what about lunch?'

She went away with chuckles of delight when Andreas told her that they were not hungry.

'We'll eat later,' he said softly, gathering Olivia back into his arms. 'Much later,' he added, his eyes darkening as he looked down at her.

'I'm hungry!' Her little wail of protest was cut short by his gentle kisses.

'So am I.' His soft laughter was against her mouth as he pulled her closer, his lips silencing her at last.

Here's how to get this special offer from Harlequin!

November
BETTY NEELS
TREASURY EDITION
COUPON

As simple as 1...2...3!

1. Each month, save one Treasury Edition coupon from your favorite Romance or Presents novel.

2. In four months you'll have saved four Treasury Edition coupons (only one coupon per month allowed).

3. Then all you have to do is fill out and return the order form provided, along with the four Treasury Edition coupons required and $2.95 for postage and handling.

BN-Nov-2

Mail to: Harlequin Reader Service

In the U.S.A.
901 Fuhrmann Blvd.
P.O. Box 1397
Buffalo, NY 14240

In Canada
P.O. Box 609
Fort Erie, Ontario
L2A 9Z9

Please send me my Special copy of the Betty Neels Treasury Edition. I have enclosed the four Treasury Edition coupons required and $2.95 for postage and handling along with this order form. (Please Print)

NAME_____

ADDRESS_____

CITY_____

STATE/PROV._____ ZIP/POSTAL CODE_____

SIGNATURE_____
This offer is limited to one order per household.

SUPPLIES LIMITED

This special Betty Neels offer expires
February 28, 1987.

Take 4 novels and a surprise gift FREE